Someone's Gonna End Up Crying

Someone's Gonna End Up Crying

JO KNOWLES

illustrated by
GLYNNIS FAWKES

CANDLEWICK PRESS

This is a work of fiction. Names, characters, places, and incidents are either products of the author's imagination or, if real, are used fictitiously.

Text copyright © 2025 by Jo Knowles
Illustrations copyright © 2025 by Glynnis Fawkes

All rights reserved. No part of this book may be reproduced, transmitted, or stored in an information retrieval system in any form or by any means, graphic, electronic, or mechanical, including photocopying, taping, and recording, without prior written permission from the publisher.

First edition 2025

Library of Congress Control Number: 2024950566
ISBN 978-1-5362-3127-4

25 26 27 28 29 30 APS 10 9 8 7 6 5 4 3 2 1

Printed in Humen, Dongguan, China

This book was typeset in Berkeley Oldstyle.
The illustrations were done in pen and ink and finished digitally.

Candlewick Press
99 Dover Street
Somerville, Massachusetts 02144

www.candlewick.com

EU Authorized Representative: HackettFlynn Ltd,
36 Cloch Choirneal, Balrothery, Co. Dublin, K32 C942, Ireland.
EU@walkerpublishinggroup.com

A JUNIOR LIBRARY GUILD SELECTION

*For Joan—
I cannot imagine a more loving editor
to have walked beside on this journey.
Thank you for everything.
JK*

*For anyone who has found solace
in cartooning.
GF*

One

Fridays are my salty days, and today I'm feeling extra spicy. My mom and dad were already arguing when I came down for breakfast, so I grabbed a piece of toast and ran out to the maple tree in our backyard to study for my weekly math quiz until it's time to leave for school. The quiz is reason number one for my bad mood. The arguing makes it worse.

Even from outside, I can hear my parents bickering about whose turn it is to go grocery shopping and whose responsibility it is to make dinner tonight and blah blah

blah. My dad always says he doesn't like conflict, but he sure has a funny way of showing it lately.

I press my head against my tree. "I wish they'd stop," I whisper.

Confession: I talk to trees.

No, that's not totally true. I only talk to *this* tree. My tree. I know it sounds silly, but I'm sure it can hear me, even if it doesn't talk back.

My mom says that when she was pregnant with me, she used to sit under this very tree and read to Gabe and Rory, my older brother and sister. She said it was the one time she could get some rest from chasing those two around. Something about the tree calmed them down, she said. Not only that, but when she sat under it, I would stop kicking inside her and settle down, too. She loved sitting under the tree and the special feeling it gave her so much, she decided to name me after it: Maple.

When I want to be alone, I come out to my tree and climb on the tire swing my dad set up when we were little, or I sit on the ground and lean against the trunk. Sometimes I draw in my sketchbook. But other times, when I'm feeling extra sad, I whisper my problems, like when my mom and dad fight and my dad goes for a drive to "cool off," and we don't know when he'll come back. Rory calls these our dad's "Space Times" because he always hollers, "I just need some space!" then takes off and leaves my mom to pace around the house and worry until he comes back.

When I tell the tree I'm scared, the leaves rustle as if to say, *I hear you, Maple. I'll do what I can.* I imagine the rustling is how it whispers to the other trees, one to the next, until they reach my dad and remind him that he loves us and that it's time to go home. That's not how it really works, of course. But my dad always *does* come back, all calmed down and acting like nothing has changed.

"Maple! Time for school!" Rory shouts at me from the back door.

"See you later," I whisper, and run around the house to the car.

"No one likes a grouchy Maple," my dad says, giving me a disapproving look in the rearview mirror as he drives us to school. He makes a face to imitate mine, which makes me even saltier. It doesn't help that Gabe and Rory have been calling out division problems at me since we got in the car.

"Twenty-seven divided by nine!" Rory yells from the front passenger seat. She's in the seventh grade and gets straight As in every subject.

"I don't need to be quizzed!" I say, still scowling.

Three.

"If Maple doesn't want you quizzing her, you need to respect her wishes," my dad says. He winks at me in the mirror. "It's just a quiz, sweetie. Don't sweat it."

"How will she ever pass if we don't quiz her?" Gabe asks. He's in the ninth grade and gets to use a fancy calculator for his math classes. I don't see why we have to memorize all these math problems if we can use a calculator in a few years.

At the start of fifth grade, my math teacher, Ms. Kent, gave the class a long lecture about how important it is to know division, not just our times tables. Every Friday, we have a quiz, and once we all "ace" it, we get to have an ice-cream party. All year long, the rest of my class has been acing quiz after quiz—except for me and Parker Diaz. Now that it's June, the pressure is on so we can still have a party before it's too late.

I know my division. I do! But there's something about the kitchen timer Ms. Kent uses to time the quiz, the *clickety-click* it makes as it counts down the seconds we have left, that jumbles all the numbers in my head. I wind up making the triangle of my four go to the right instead of the left, and while I'm busy erasing my mistake, the timer goes off with its piercing ring. Then everyone groans because they can tell I blew it again.

My mom wanted to tell Ms. Kent the quiz was

stressing some kids out, but I begged her not to, and my dad agreed she should stay out of it. Then he and my mom got in an argument and forgot all about what the issue was in the first place. They hardly ever used to argue, but lately it seems they disagree about everything.

Rory rolls down her window and leans way out, her seat belt stretching with her. She opens her mouth and sticks out her tongue like a dog. "Feel the breeeeeeeze!" she shouts, leaning farther out. "Ar-arhoooo!" she yelps like a dog.

It's a good thing my mom isn't driving us because she would not be happy with this behavior. Usually, when we kids do something my mom thinks either is dangerous or will end up with us fighting, she has a saying she sings as a way to warn us to stop:

"Someone's gonna end up cry-ing!"

She always sing-yells it instead of just yelling. And she's almost always right.

But today, my dad is driving. Instead of reaching over to pull Rory back in, he rolls down his own window, leans his head out, and shouts, "Yeah! Arhoooo!"

When we slow down and stop at a traffic light, Rory leans back in. "No wonder dogs do that all the time! Try it, Maple! It'll help you release some stress!"

When the light turns green, my dad guns it to pick up speed. I roll down my window and poke my head out. The morning air is still cold, even though it's almost summer.

"Open your mouth and stick out your tongue!" Rory tells me.

I do as she says and feel the air fill my mouth, cool and damp from the late spring dew.

Suddenly, something sharp hits my tongue! I shriek and shoot my head back inside the car.

"What happened?" Gabe asks.

I touch my tongue. Whatever hit me is still there!

"It's a bug!" I holler, then spit it onto my hand.

Rory turns in her seat and leans toward me to inspect the bug bits. "Was that a ladybug? They bring good luck! I mean, unless you kill it with your tongue. Then it's probably bad luck."

"At least you didn't swallow it," Gabe says. "Who knows what kind of disease it could give you."

"Or maybe you could have gotten superpowers," Rory says. "Like when Peter Parker gets bitten by a spider and becomes Spider-Man! I wonder what kind of superpowers a ladybug would have."

"It hurts!" I touch my tongue. What if a piece of bug *did* get inside me, and I get some horrible bug disease? "Dad! Pull over! I'm going to be sick!"

"Oh, relax and don't be such a baby," Gabe says.

If there is one thing I do not like to be told to do, it is to relax, especially when I'm upset. And if there is one thing I don't like to be called, it's a baby. He knows this. Everyone in my family knows this.

I reach over and wipe the back of my hand on his arm, smearing my spit and the dead bug on his bare skin.

"Maple! You're so disgusting!" He wipes his arm on the back of Rory's seat.

"Maybe now *you'll* get a superpower," I say.

"I wish you kids wouldn't fight," my dad says. "Life's too short to waste it on being mad."

My dad is always saying stuff like that. I wish he would take his own advice, though, because it seems like he gets mad at my mom all the time.

I lean back and close my eyes and try to go through my division problems in my head, forcing myself to write the numbers perfectly on the first try. Instead, I start to see a comic about a girl who turns into a kid-size ladybug. I sit up, reach in my backpack for my sketchbook, and start to draw.

"You're going to get carsick doing that," Gabe says in his know-it-all tone.

I ignore him and scribble my ideas down, carefully leaning over the pages so he can't see.

I smile to myself, imagining my new superhero identity and what I would do if I could fly. PLUS, I'd have a cool shell that would protect me. PLUS, I'd bring good luck to people!

As I'm doodling away, I don't realize we've pulled up to my school. My dad stops the car and turns around. "You've got this, kiddo. Go tell that quiz who's boss."

I shove my sketchbook back into my bag.

"Forty-two divided by seven!" Gabe says.

I roll my eyes at him.

Six.

"Don't take the test, Maple," Rory says as I open my door to get out. "Take a stand!"

"Sixty-four divided by eight!" Gabe says.

"Just do your best!" my dad says.

I get out and slam my door.

Eight.

"We love you," my dad says through his open window.

"Fight the power!" Rory calls as I walk up the sidewalk toward the main entrance. She leans out the window and pants like a dog. "Ar-arhoooo!"

I roll my eyes again and keep walking.

Two

"Maple! Maple! Wait up!" Katy and Astrid, my best friends, run toward me holding hands. They always do this when they see me because one time when we were watching an adventure movie, I pointed out how silly it was for the characters to hold hands and run during a chase scene. Why would anyone in real life do that when they could run so much faster if they could swing both arms? Katy and Astrid said maybe it's because they didn't want to be separated. We never could agree. But whenever we run, they grab my hands so we won't lose one another.

"Happy Friday!" Astrid says, taking my hand with her free one.

We walk along, swinging our arms.

"Ready for the quiz?" Astrid asks.

"Don't remind me."

"You can do it this time!" Katy says.

I know she's just trying to be encouraging, but it annoys me, like she's saying I just need to try harder. I have tried. All year.

When we get to class, Parker is already sitting at his desk, studying.

"Morning, girls. Take a seat," Ms. Kent says.

As soon as I sit, I start to fidget. I look at the clock, then down at my desk. I hope we take the quiz first thing so I can just get it over with. Instead, Ms. Kent tells us she'll give us five minutes to review silently before the quiz. Ugh. I spot the timer on the corner of her desk. I wish I could be Captain Ladybug. I'd swoop over, snatch that timer, and fly away with it. I'd whoosh down the hall and out the big glass doors at the front of the school. All the kids would open their classroom windows and cheer for me. "Go, go, Captain Ladybug!" they'd holler, and I'd flash them a smile before I flew up, uP, UP, and AWAY!

"Quiz time!" Ms. Kent sings.

I quickly shut my sketchbook and hope Ms. Kent didn't see me using study time to draw.

Ms. Kent walks around the room putting a slip of paper on everyone's desk, facedown. Then she goes to the front of the room and picks up the timer.

"Ready, set, go!" she says.

We flip over our papers, and she turns the timer to start. The clickety-clicking already sets me on edge.

Question one: Eighty-one divided by nine.

Nine.

I make the head of the nine, then a tail down. One question down, nineteen to go.

Question two: Fifty-six divided by eight.

Seven.

Click-click-click-click-click.

I try to block out the noise and continue on, one question after the other. My dad says slow and steady wins the race. But that's not true in this case.

"*Brinngggggg!*" And just like that, time's up.

"Maple!" Astrid whispers from her desk beside me. "How'd you do?"

I look down at two still unanswered questions and frown.

Ms. Kent walks up and down the rows of desks,

picking up the quizzes. Her shoes shuffle-shuffle with each step.

I glance over at Parker, and we exchange a look. It's our "messed up again" look.

Ms. Kent pauses at my desk and reaches for my paper. I imagine I'm Captain Ladybug and burn the answers to the last two questions onto the paper with my laser eyes. *Eight! Six!*

"You're getting closer, Maple," she says. "Great job!"

The class groans.

"Uh-uh!" Ms. Kent says to shush them. But even though they stop, I know inside they are all still groaning.

Three

Rory, Gabe, and I take the school bus home in the afternoons because my parents are still working when school gets out. I always sit with Astrid in the fourth row. Astrid is kind and doesn't bring up the quiz. Instead, we talk about plans for summer vacation, which is almost here. Astrid lives three streets over from me, and we spend the summer at each other's houses as much as possible. Katy lives a little bit farther away, but she rides her bike to see us. Most days, we hang out in

Astrid's clubhouse because it has a door that locks and no one can bother us, especially not the ABC's, also known as the Jensen triplets, who live next door to her. Their real names are Adam, Bryce, and Charlie, and they are *trouble*.

"My dad promised he'd help me make a tree fort this summer," I tell Astrid. "So we'll have two places to hide out!"

"Didn't he promise you that last summer?" Astrid asks.

"Yeah, but he got busy with work," I say. I can tell my voice sounds funny, as if something got in my throat. It does that when I get sad all of a sudden. My dad makes a lot of promises that don't always come true. Usually, he blames it on his job and having to work late, or being too tired after a stressful day. When this happens, my mom gets upset and points out that she works, too, but she still fulfills *her* promises. And when *that* happens, my dad gets mad at my mom. And that's when the arguing starts. Either that, or my dad storms off somewhere to avoid arguing, which only makes things worse.

"Sorry," Astrid says. "I didn't mean to make you feel bad."

I look out the window, away from her. "Tree forts take lots of planning," I say. "The tree I have in mind is special. If I'm going to build a fort in it, I want it to be perfect."

"Better make sure the ABC's can't break into it." Astrid looks over her shoulder to see if they're listening. They always sit squished together in the sixth row, across the aisle from their younger sister, Dora. She's in the first grade and seems like the opposite of the triplets. Quiet. Thoughtful. And not up to trouble.

"Anyway," Astrid goes on in a quieter voice, "I highly recommend a trapdoor."

"I'm going to ask for a rope ladder. Then we can pull it up behind us, and no one will be able to climb up!"

"Brilliant!"

I pull my sketchbook out of my bag. I don't usually show anyone my drawings, but I want to show Astrid the plans I made for my fort. That's different from showing her my comics.

I open to the back of my book and show her my sketch.

"Impressive!" Astrid says. "I wish I could draw like you."

"You can! I'll teach you!"

"In the fort? Over the summer?"

"Yes!" I put my sketchbook away, feeling much better.

The bus's brakes screech at the next stop, and the ABC's and Dora walk past before Astrid can get out. One of them trips as they walk by and bumps into me, knocking my backpack off my lap.

"Sorry!" he says. But I bet it was on purpose.

Astrid rolls her eyes. "I know my mom says they're good boys, but I beg to differ."

Astrid always says things like "I beg to differ" and other stuff adults say. She's an only child and talks just like her parents, which is one of my favorite things about her.

"Agreed," I say, making room for Astrid to step into the aisle.

"I'll call to let you know when I can come over this weekend," Astrid says over her shoulder as she follows the ABC's off the bus.

When we get to my stop, I race Gabe and Rory up the driveway. Rory wins, as usual. She throws her stuff on the floor inside the door and hurries to the kitchen to make a snack.

We have a little rack in the entryway that has a hook for each of us to hang our coats on and a shelf for our shoes. We're supposed to take our backpacks to our rooms. Our house is really small, so we have to keep things tidy or else it gets cluttered and messy pretty quickly. But Rory isn't the type to care about clutter or messes.

I put my and Rory's things away properly, then find her and Gabe in the kitchen.

"Well?" they both ask me.

"What?" I ask.

"The quiz!" Rory says. "Did you ace it?"

I shake my head. I'd kind of put that behind me, but as soon as they mention it, I feel annoyed all over again.

"Oh well, better luck next time," Rory says. "Here, have a chip."

I take a potato chip from the bowl she's holding and make a big crunch when I bite it.

A sour taste stings my tongue. "Ack!" I throw the rest of the chip back in the bowl.

"Gross!" Gabe says, doing the same. "What kind of chips are these?"

"My new specialty," Rory says. "We only had plain, so I put some salt and vinegar on them to liven things up." She fishes through the bowl as if each chip would taste different, then puts one in her mouth. She scrunches up her face the second the flavor hits her.

"Maybe not my best invention," she says.

"When are Mom and Dad getting home?" I ask. "And what's for dinner?"

We look for the notepad that Dad leaves messages on to see if we're supposed to do any chores or help get dinner ready. Sometimes he asks us to make a salad. Or sometimes we have to get something out of the freezer. But when we find the pad, it still has yesterday's note.

"Maybe he forgot," I say. "Should we text and ask?"

"No way!" Rory says. "Why add work for ourselves when we don't have to? Besides, maybe he's bringing home takeout for a surprise!"

"Why would he do that?" Gabe asks. "There's nothing important happening today."

Usually, we get takeout only for special occasions. And we get to go to restaurants only on *really* special occasions. Neither of my parents makes a lot of money at their jobs. My mom is an administrative assistant at our community college, and my dad works as a sales rep for a solar panel company.

"Well, who knows," Rory says. "But it's Friday! And we don't have any chores, and we don't have to do homework. What should we do?"

Gabe takes another bite of a chip and makes a face. "You really overdid it with the vinegar. Way to waste an entire bag of chips."

"I'm going to eat them!" Rory says. "Just . . . very slowly."

Four

"Let's go see the Ganders," I say after we give up on the chips. That's what we call Salt and Pepper, the two geese who live next door at our neighbors' house.

We run outside and race to the back of our property to where our neighbors' land begins. I love that Gabe and Rory still act like kids sometimes and play with me and want to have adventures.

Gabe makes a honking noise, and we all wait at the wooden fence that separates our properties. Sure enough, there's a rustling in the bushes, and Salt comes waddling toward us at top speed, followed close behind by Pepper. Salt is all white, but Pepper has a few black specks on the top of his head.

"Hey, Salty!" Rory says as he continues charging. "Whoa, boy!"

Salt honks at us like a dog protecting its territory. In the distance, one of the donkeys who also lives next door brays back as if it's saying thank you for guarding him. The donkeys' names are Hero and Daisy. They're kept in a corral attached to the barn, so they can't come say hello.

"Salt is saltier than ever," I say. "Too bad we can't give him snacks. I bet he'd like us a lot more."

Gabe and I look at Rory and roll our eyes. She's the reason we're not allowed to give the Ganders snacks anymore.

"How was I supposed to know geese can't eat french fries?" Rory says. "I was just trying to be generous. Besides, neither of them even got sick! The Lloyds are just paranoid."

"Because they love their pets," I point out.

Pepper reaches his head through the fence and tries to bite my knee.

• • •

After a while, the geese get bored with us and start to forage in the weeds for bugs. We climb up on the fence and sit to watch.

"Have you guys noticed that Mom and Dad have been different lately?" Rory asks.

Gabe shifts on the fence. "Different how?"

"More arguments?" I ask.

Rory nods. "Dad's so touchy. It seems like he uses any excuse to get mad at Mom and leave in a huff."

When I get mad and don't want to talk to anyone, I like to draw or go talk to my tree. I wish Dad did that instead of storming off and not saying where he's going.

"We haven't had a family game night in forever," Rory says. "And Mom and Dad never play music when they make dinner anymore. Actually, I can't even remember the last time they made dinner together. They used to love to do that."

"You worry too much," Gabe says. "They're just busy. And Dad's job is really stressful, trying to find new clients all the time to meet his monthly sales quota."

"Maybe," Rory says. "I guess."

Salt and Pepper come back to where we're sitting on the fence and try to peck our toes.

"Geese are weird," Gabe says.

"But good guards," I say.

"But are they?" Rory asks. "I mean, a honking goose doesn't seem nearly as scary as a growling dog. Besides, all they can do is peck at you. How much could that hurt?"

"Let's find out," Gabe says. "I dare you to jump down and run to the barn and back. You have to tap the barn door with your hand."

"Are you faster than a goose?" I ask Rory.

She studies them. "I mean, look at their webbed feet and how short their legs are. You really think I can't outrun them?"

"But they have wings and you don't," Gabe points out. "So there's that."

Rory hops to the ground and flaps her arms as if she has wings, too, and she's ready to take flight. If there's one thing Gabe, Rory, and I have in common, it's the trouble we have turning down a dare, no matter how challenging.

Salt and Pepper immediately start honking at her.

"Someone's gonna end up cry-ing," I sing under my breath in my best impression of our mom.

Rory gets into a start position, ready to race.

"On your mark . . ." Gabe says.

"Get set . . ." I add.

"Go!" we shout at the same time.

Rory dashes toward the barn full speed ahead. Salt and Pepper look confused at first, as if they're trying to decide whether one of them should stay here and guard me and Gabe or if they should both go after Rory. They quickly decide to charge after her and half run, half fly, their wings flapping wildly. I've never heard them squawk so loudly!

Rory gets to the barn before they do and taps it triumphantly, but when she turns and sees the Ganders zooming toward her, her grin is replaced by a look of terror.

I jump down from the fence. "Don't run!" I yell. "They're going to attack you!"

Rory freezes, but the geese don't let up. She darts to the left, then to the right, but when they reach her, they start pecking like mad.

"Ow! Ow! Get off me!" she squeals.

In the distance, Hero and Daisy join the chorus, hee-hawing in panic.

"We have to distract them!" I shout at Gabe.

We both run toward Rory, waving our arms.

"Hey, Salt! Come and get me!" I shout. I turn and wiggle my bum at the geese to try to lure them away from Rory. My mom told us when someone pinches you there, it's called a "goose" because that's what geese do.

Salt and Pepper stop and turn.

"It's working!" Gabe says. He waves his arms in the air again and runs in another direction, staying near the fence so he can hop over it if they get too close.

Rory sees her chance and makes a run for it the other way. The Ganders are so confused, they start squabbling with each other. All three of us run back to the fence and scramble over it to safety.

"YES!" Rory says. And then, "Ow!" when she realizes her legs are covered in little welts.

The Ganders honk at Rory from the other side of the fence.

"Can't get me!" she sings, then sticks her tongue out at them.

"You know they could get over this fence if they really wanted to, right?" Gabe asks.

The Ganders look at him as if he just gave them an idea.

"We should probably get out of here," I say.

We race back to the house, and of course Rory wins. We sit on the back steps to catch our breath.

Rory inspects her welts and grumbles.

"Serves you right, really," Gabe points out.

"They were just doing their job," I add.

"I still won," Rory says. "So it was worth it."

"You only won because we distracted them!" I say.

"But I still won." Rory holds up her arms to make muscles. "Champion!"

"Too bad there aren't any medals for outrunning geese," Gabe says in his sarcastic way.

After we cool off, I go inside and get out my sketchbook and turn our adventure into a comic. I think it's my best one yet!

Five

My mom gets home around dinnertime, but she hasn't brought any food with her.

"Where's your father?" she asks. "Did he leave a note about what to get out for dinner?"

We shake our heads.

She frowns, looking annoyed. "Ah, well. What should we make?" She reaches across the counter to where Rory's bowl of homemade salt-and-vinegar chips sits mostly uneaten and takes one.

"Mom, those are—" I start to say, but it's too late.

She makes a horrified face and gags. "What did you kids do to these chips?!"

Even though the three of us don't always get along,

we never *ever* tell on each other or, as Rory says, "rat each other out."

Gabe and I shrug, but Rory must feel bad because she confesses.

"They're my invention," she says. "Salt-and-Vinegar Extreme."

My mom pours herself a glass of water and drinks half of it. "More like Extra Extreme."

"Sorry," Rory tells her. "I'll eat them so they don't go to waste."

"It's OK," my mom says. "Just . . . next time start with a small amount before you waste an entire bag of chips."

She gets busy pulling stuff out of the fridge to see what she can throw together for dinner.

Another hour goes by and my dad still isn't home. My mom manages to make a big salad with weird stuff in it. "Everything but the Kitchen Sink Salad," she says.

The bowl sits on the counter, waiting for my dad. Since it's Friday night and we don't have homework, my mom tries to keep us busy by offering to play a game.

We decide on Uno, and eventually it's down to me against Gabe. My pile is the biggest when we're interrupted by the sound of the front door creaking open.

In walks Dad, all cheerful. "Hey, guys!" he says, as if it's perfectly normal to show up so late without telling anyone where he's been. "Whatcha playing?"

"Uno!" Gabe tells him, acting just as normal. "And Maple's only winning because she cheats!"

"I do not!" I do *not* cheat. Ever! Gabe knows this and is just trying to get my goat. It works.

"Calm down and finish up so we can set the table," my mom says.

I can't stand being told to calm down, especially when I have every right to be upset!

"What's for dinner?" my dad asks as he walks into the kitchen. "Wow! That's a big salad!"

Before my mom turns to follow him, I see a look of anger on her face. It's the look she gets when one of us *does* end up crying, because we did something we should have known better than to do. But it's more than anger, really. There's a mixture of disappointment there, too. Or sadness.

Gabe says he forfeits, and we clean up the cards without finishing the game. The three of us try to be quiet as we set the table so we can hear what our parents are talking about, but they're too good at knowing how to be private.

"This is the calm before the storm," Rory says. "Right?"

"Shhh," Gabe whispers. "You don't know that."

"I hate it when they fight," I say under my breath.

"They aren't fighting." Gabe puts a napkin next to each plate. "Not yet, anyway."

"Should we go in and see if they want help?" Rory asks quietly. "Maybe if we distract them, Mom will forget she's mad."

"Just sit and wait." As Gabe pulls out his chair to sit down, our parents' voices start to rise, as if they're getting into an argument.

"Let's go watch something," Gabe says.

"But what about dinner?" I ask. "I'm hungry!"

"You'll live," Gabe says.

"Maybe Dad's just upset because he tried one of the chips," Rory says. "Shouldn't we wait for them?"

We wait a few more minutes. There's a lot of "How hard is it to text me to say you're working late, Dan?" and "I didn't realize you were my keeper, Colleen!" and a bunch of other mean things, and then finally "Fine!" and "Fine!" before they get quiet again. They stroll out into the dining room as if nothing happened, my mom carrying the big salad bowl and my dad trying to hold three different salad dressing bottles in one hand and the gross bowl of chips in the other.

We all sit down and take turns passing the salad bowl around. I try to carefully pick through the mixture of lettuce, chopped veggies, and random nuts and croutons my mom tossed in to make it count as a meal.

"Hurry up, Maple! And stop taking all the good stuff!" Rory says, elbowing me.

"Don't bicker," my dad says. "Looks like your mom threw plenty of stuff in there for everyone." He smiles at my mom as if to say *I'm sorry* and *Thank you* at the same time. I hope that means they made up.

After Rory puts a heaping pile of salad on her plate, she takes a big handful of chips and crushes them up with her fingers over the top.

"Gross!" Gabe says.

"There's vinegar in salad dressing—what's the difference?" She makes a point of taking a big bite and crunching the chips at Gabe. "Delicious!"

My mom reaches for a handful of the chips and copies Rory, which is kind of shocking because she doesn't usually do stuff like that. Part of me wants to add some chips, too, just to support them. But the chips really are pretty terrible, and I'm too hungry to ruin my salad.

My mom makes a big deal of taking a bite and acting as if it's the best salad topping ever invented, but I notice she also takes an extra-long drink of water.

• • •

After dinner, instead of playing a family game or watching a movie together, like we usually do on Friday nights, everyone goes off to do their own thing. My dad sits in the chair that faces the window, even though it's too dark to see anything outside. My mom takes a book upstairs to read in bed. Gabe plays some game on his phone, and Rory texts a friend and disappears upstairs.

    I find my sketchbook and get comfy on the couch. Even though everyone's home, it feels lonely. I don't like it when they all want to do their own thing. We do our own things all week! Weekends are supposed to be for family time. But it seems like no one wants to be together, especially not my mom and dad.

THE BORINGS!

Six

"Morning, Mapes," my dad says when I wander downstairs to the kitchen the next morning. "Want some coffee?"

I make a face. "Not today," I say. I pour myself some water and find Rory in the living room. She's watching *Avatar: The Last Airbender*. We've seen it at least fifteen times. It's our favorite show, and we know practically all the lines.

I settle next to her on the couch with my sketchbook. I love to draw while we watch, making my own scenes based on the show.

Rory pauses the show. "If you could have a bending power, would it be earth, fire, water, or air?" she asks.

"We've had this conversation a thousand times," I say.

"I know, but you could always change your mind."

My favorite character is Toph, the earthbender, because she's small, like me, and makes funny jokes. She's also sassy and tough, which I'm not but wish I was sometimes.

"Can we start with the skill we wouldn't want?" I ask.

"Fine."

"OK, then, earthbending."

"But that's one of the most effective ones! Why wouldn't you want to earthbend?"

Even though Toph is my favorite, I don't think I'd want to be able to move the earth and push giant rocks around and stuff.

"C'mon," Rory says. "I can tell you have a reason."

"You'll roll your eyes," I say.

Rory rolls her eyes a lot. She says I "exasperate" her with my logic.

"I don't like the idea of disturbing things," I say.

Rory makes her exasperated face. I knew it.

"Why not?"

"Nature shouldn't be disturbed. Like, what if there's a reason there are rocks in a certain place? You know, like when we help Dad in the yard, sometimes we find ants under the rocks. It disturbs their home!"

"Oh, Maple."

"What?"

"It's just a game. It's not like we'd *actually* get powers. Just let yourself daydream for once!"

"For once? I daydream all the time!" I would point out that my sketchbook is filled with comics that illustrate all my daydreams, but there's no way I'm sharing my private drawings with her. My sketchbook is like a diary. The comics I make are just for me. In my head, though, I think about Captain Ladybug and smirk to myself.

"Fine. OK, which is your next least favorite?" Rory asks.

"Fire."

"WHAT?! That's even more powerful than earthbending!"

"I know and that's why! I don't want to burn things! What if I started a forest fire?"

"Oh, Maple."

"Water is next. I don't think any animals would get hurt from making waves and splashing water around. But water is precious, so I wouldn't want to waste it."

"Sheesh, you sure know how to take the fun out of this."

I hate it when Rory says stuff like that. I'm fun! I just care about things.

"Air is the best," I say. "You can fly! You can keep the

bad guys away just by blowing wind at them. And wind doesn't disturb nature too much, especially if you're careful about not blowing over flowers and plants and things."

"You'd be the most boring superhero ever," Rory says.

"I would not!" I lift up my hand and spread my fingers out the way Aang does in the show when he airbends. I make a serious face, as if I'm going to blow air at Rory and send her whooshing across the room.

She rolls her eyes again and starts the show back up. As we watch, every time someone uses a skill, I point out the damage it could cause to the environment, and Rory gets so annoyed, she leaves the room. As soon as she's gone, I start a new comic.

"Whatcha doin'?" my dad asks.

I quickly shut my book and turn around on the couch, which he is perched behind. He was obviously trying to look over my shoulder, even though he knows this book is private. That's not like him.

"Nothing," I say, annoyed.

"Sorry, Mapes. I didn't see anything." But the point is, I think he tried.

"You ready for breakfast? It's been a while since we had my Saturday Smorgasbord Special." My dad's Smorgasbord Special is a lot like my mom's Everything but the Kitchen Sink Salad. Basically, it's taking whatever cereal and "mix-ins" we have in the cupboard and putting them all out in little bowls on the counter for people to make their own creations, like a salad bar, but a cereal bar instead.

"OK," I say. "Let me put my stuff away first."

"Great! I'll go get started." He kisses the top of my head and sashays back into the kitchen. That's what he calls the silly walk-dance he does when he's in a good mood. I guess he's going to pretend nothing happened last night and all is forgiven. Sometimes, I wish my dad would at least apologize when he does things that are inconsiderate, especially to my mom. But he always acts as though my mom is the one who was overreacting and making him feel bad. I guess I should just be glad he and my mom aren't still fighting.

Upstairs, I walk down the tiny hall to my room, which used to be a big linen closet. I shared a room with Rory when we were younger, but then my parents decided (and Rory begged) to let her have her own space and made me this mini one. There is almost no room in it besides my tiny bed, which used to be a shelf! I won't be able to fit here much longer. When I sleep, I can already touch my toes to the wall. But the great thing about having a shelf for a bed is that it's kind of like having a multilevel bunk bed. There are three shelves: on the top is where I put my books, games, and private things, like my sketchbook; on the middle is my bed; and then on the bottom is a row of bins where I put my clothes and things.

I'm not sure what I'll do when I get too big for the closet, though. Rory wants my parents to build a tiny house in the backyard that we kids can live in. When my parents said we were too young for our own house, we told them they could sleep out there, and the three of us could have the upstairs to ourselves. But my mom didn't think that was the best idea in the world, either. Maybe I'll just have to sleep in my future tree fort.

But for now, when I have friends for sleepovers, we

sleep on the floor in the living room. We make blanket forts across the couch and coffee table and stay up late. I'm kind of glad my room is too small for guests because blanket forts are the best. Besides, this way, my room is all mine. It's my special place that no one else is allowed in, and even if they wanted to come in, they couldn't fit!

After I put my sketchbook away, I go back downstairs and join my dad in the kitchen. He has some music playing, and he sways back and forth at the counter, bobbing his head.

"Maple!" he says when he notices me. He shakes two cereal boxes as if they're maracas and wiggles his hips, then hands me one.

"Bad news, pal," he tells me. "We only have four types of cereal."

"It's the mix-ins that count," I say.

"Right!" He turns and gestures to the bowls he's put out on the counter. There's some honey, a bag of coconut flakes, some raisins, sunflower seeds, and a bunch of other healthy-looking stuff I don't like as much.

I nod anyway. "It'll do."

He smiles and gives me a hug. His breath smells like coffee, which is not a good smell. But his old T-shirt is soft against my face and feels nice. I wrap my arms around his squishy waist and squeeze, and he squeezes back.

"Is it Smorgasbord Saturday?" Rory asks, walking into the kitchen.

"What's it look like?" I ask.

She rolls her eyes at me. Someday they are going to get stuck up there, just like my mom says.

"When's breakfast?" she asks.

"Now!" my dad says. "Time to wake up the sleepyheads." We follow him out to the stairs.

"Riiiiiiiiise and shiiiiiiiiiine!" he sings like an opera singer.

Rory and I set the table and get out milk and juice. My dad and I love orange juice, but Rory, Gabe, and my mom drink only milk. I have a hard time with milk ever since I went on a field trip to a farm with my school. We learned to milk cows and collect eggs and do a bunch of other farm-y stuff, and it was all a little weird. Ever since then, I think a lot about where my food comes from. And who it comes from. I can't get the image of the cow's udder out of my head when I pour a glass of milk. Or the smell of the barn. And when I crack an egg, I can't help thinking that it came out of a chicken! Rory makes fun of me for being so squeamish.

"You overthink everything, Maple," she says every time I have trouble. "That's your problem. You need to stop thinking about every little thing."

My mom gets after her when she says things like

this. That's because my mom is a lot like me. She knows what it feels like when someone tells you to stop being so serious or that you're no fun. I've heard my dad say that to her a bunch of times, and whenever he does, she always looks hurt. And that's how I feel, too.

Rory never seems to overthink anything. She just goes with the flow without a care, just like my dad. That's part of the problem. They don't always seem to care about how their actions might affect other people. That's why Rory ends up getting nearly pecked to death by guard geese! But, I admit, it can also lead to lots of fun.

Seven

On Monday morning, we all pile in the car again. It's Gabe's turn to sit in the front seat, and he insists on blasting his playlist. Everyone sings along and it feels nice, like we're heading out on a fun road trip and not going to school. Rory rolls down her window and sings to the world as we drive by. My dad uses the controls to roll down the rest of our windows, then turns the music up even louder. He and Gabe stick their heads out the window like Rory and sing at the top of their lungs, even though they can't carry a tune. I'm too embarrassed to join in.

"C'mon, Maple, live a little!" Rory says, elbowing me.

"Yeah!" Gabe and my dad say.

I know perfectly well how to live! I just don't like drawing attention to myself. I can't stand it when they say things like that to me. Like when they call me a party pooper or a stick-in-the-mud whenever I don't want to do something that brings attention to myself. They're always doing stuff that says "Look at us! We know how to have fun! We don't care what anyone thinks!" They are the types who not only will always pick dare in Truth or Dare but will take whatever dare it is one step further! One time, when we were playing with the neighborhood kids, Rory was dared to run around the neighborhood wearing our old dress-up clothes. She had a monster mask and silver shoes, but that wasn't enough for Rory! She searched through the dress-up trunk and found a bright purple feather boa, a pirate hat, and fairy wings and pranced through the neighborhood singing "Let It Go"! Neighbors came out of their houses, and the kids all followed behind her as if she was the queen of the neighborhood. That's just how Rory is.

But me? Not so much. I'm more like my mom. My dad said she and I are wallflowers. It means we are too shy to fit in, so we try to blend in with the walls at parties and other gatherings. Something like that. When he told me what it meant, I drew a whole series of self-portraits of me at all the places I don't feel comfortable, blending

into the walls. I thought they were pretty funny, but when I shared them with my dad, he got a sad look on his face and ruffled my hair, then hugged me close.

"I hope you won't always want to hide yourself, Maple. Everyone should know how special you are."

"Like Mom?" I asked him.

He squeezed me tighter. "Yeah. She's pretty special, too."

Still, his disappointment in my drawings is just another reason I don't like showing my work to anyone.

When I get to school, Katy and Astrid are outside waiting for me, as usual. We grab hands and start to run up the walk until Mr. Sanchez, our gym teacher, tells us to slow down.

"We're getting in our daily calisthenics, Mr. Sanchez!" Astrid says.

"Don't be sassy," Mr. Sanchez says. But he grins and does three squats right in the middle of the sidewalk. "Give me five!"

Astrid drops our hands and starts to bend her knees to do a squat.

"Oh brother," says Katy, and joins her.

I'm super embarrassed but don't want to draw more attention by being the only one not to do it.

"One!" Mr. Sanchez shouts. "Two! Three! Four! Five! Well done, girls! Now get to class."

Astrid skips ahead of us. She is always full of energy. Katy takes a deep breath and nudges me with her elbow. "What are calisthenics again?" she asks.

"You know," I say. "That's what Mr. Sanchez calls exercise."

"Ohhhhhh," she says.

She skips away to catch up to Astrid.

I am not a skipper. At least not in public. I speed-walk until I catch up, and then the three of us hurry to our lockers, which are all in the same small section near the front of the school.

"Hey!" Astrid says. "Did one of you put this here?" She holds out a yellow envelope.

"Not me," I say.

"Nope." Katy opens her locker, and a similar yellow envelope falls out.

I open mine and find one, too. We all tear them open and find a birthday invitation from Oliver Kendall. Oliver is in our grade, and we've known him since kindergarten. He gets dressed up to come to school every day. A lot of times, he even wears a tie!

Before we can discuss, the bell rings to warn us we need to get to class.

All through my morning classes, I think about the invitation waiting in my locker. Oliver Kendall invited me to his birthday party? But we're hardly friends!

Also, he's one of the people who always gives me a disappointed look when I fail the math quiz on Fridays. Why would he want me to come to his party? Maybe he had to invite everyone. That would explain it. When I was little, my parents made me invite every kid in my class to my birthday parties, even if I didn't like them all. "You need to be inclusive, Maple," my mom always said. "How would you feel if your friends got invited to a party but you didn't?"

Of course I would feel terrible. So every year I had to invite all the kids in my class, including the ABC's, who one time opened my presents while everyone was playing outside and pretended that all the toys were theirs. Luckily, the other kids at the party recognized the presents they'd brought for me. After that, my mom suggested I have smaller parties, with just two friends, and we would do something super special, like go to Magic Mountain, which is an outdoor park that has an alpine slide you have to take a chairlift to get to. I always chose Katy and Astrid, of course. My birthday isn't for a few more weeks, but I'm already trying to decide where we should go.

"So what are you going to get Oliver for his birthday?" Astrid asks me on the bus ride home.

"I'm not sure," I say. "The invitation said it's an Office-Themed Party. What does that mean?"

"I think he wants office supplies. Maybe he needs them to fill that briefcase he brings to school every day."

"Is that what that is? I just thought it was some sort of case for his laptop."

"No, he got it from his mom," Astrid says. "She runs a business, and Oliver wants to be just like her."

"Oh. So what does he keep in his briefcase?"

"I asked him once, and he told me it was top secret information about his business."

"Wait. He has a business, too? But he's only in the fifth grade!"

Astrid shrugs. "I guess so. He told me he was a . . . hang on. It's a big word." She closes her eyes to think. This is how Astrid remembers things. "Entrepreneur!"

"What's that mean?"

"I think it's like an inventor. He also said he hired some other kids to work for him."

"Doing what?"

"He wouldn't tell me! But I know that Denzel Watson works for him. He had an Employee of the Month sticker on his shirt a couple of weeks ago, and when I asked him what it was for, he told me Oliver had given it to him."

"Wow."

"I'm thinking of getting Oliver a cashbox that locks," Astrid says. "My mom uses one when she sells crafts at the Winter Bazaar."

"Sounds expensive."

"I'll check. I'm going to ask my mom to take me to Staples to find a present before Saturday. Wanna come?"

"Yes!"

At home that night, when I tell my parents I want to buy Oliver office supplies for his birthday, they think it's cute. My dad offers to bring home some stuff from where he works, but I tell him it needs to be new.

"Well, I might be able to sneak out a ream of office paper," he says.

"Dad! That's stealing!" I can't believe he'd do such a thing.

He ruffles my hair and laughs like I'm overreacting in some sort of hilarious way.

"Glad we raised such an honest kid," he says.

My mom looks annoyed. "Of course we did," she says. "What kind of office supplies do you think he needs, Maple?"

"I don't know. He already has a briefcase, and Astrid wants to get him a cashbox."

"Maybe you should get him a stress ball!" Gabe says.

"What the heck is that?" I really don't have a clue about office supplies.

"It's a little ball you squeeze when you're stressed out."

"I don't think Oliver gets stressed," I say. "Maybe I could get him a pen?"

"People don't seem to use pens these days," my mom says. "Everyone takes notes on their phones or uses dictation."

"So I guess he won't need paper, either," my dad says.

"You both work in offices," I point out to my parents. "What kinds of stuff do you use?"

"Laptops," they say at the same time.

"I can't afford that!"

"Maybe you could get him a coffee mug," Gabe says. "That's something working people all seem to need."

"Yeah!" Rory agrees. "Get one with a saying on it, like 'World's Greatest Boss.' Something for him to aspire to!"

"Good one, Ror," my dad says.

I can't tell if they are serious or just making fun of Oliver, but it's clear they aren't really going to help me. Personally, I still think a pen is the best choice. And I'm not just saying that because I can't imagine life without one!

Eight

A few days later, Astrid, Katy, and I walk the giant aisles of Staples. Astrid's mom dropped us off and said we had thirty minutes to find something and meet her at the front door.

"Who knew there was more than one kind of paper?" Katy asks, reading all the different choices as we walk along the paper row. "One hundred percent recycled, fifty percent recycled, laser, multiuse, multipurpose—wait. What's the difference between multiuse and multipurpose? And why would you buy something that wasn't recycled?"

"Beats me," Astrid says.

"I'm going to look for a nice pen," I finally say, leaving them as they inspect the paper. "I'll find you when I choose one."

I wander off to the pen aisle and look for my favorite: Sharpies. I love the way the tip of the pen nearly sinks into the thick paper in my sketchbook. It's permanent, so if you make a mistake, it's too bad. But my comics are just for me, so it's OK if they aren't perfect. When I mess up, I turn the page into a practice page. I love to draw the same figure over and over until I come up with the right look. Then I work on their expressions.

My mom gave me a cartooning book for Christmas two years ago, and I do all the exercises. Maybe someday, I could be a famous graphic novelist. That's my secret wish. Secret because I've never told anyone my dream. Not even Astrid or Katy.

Rory wants to be a gym teacher when she grows up because she loves inventing games. Gabe likes to remind her that most of the games she invents end up with someone crying, just like Mom says. But Rory just shrugs it off and says her games are still in the testing stage.

When I get to the gel pen section, there's a piece of paper to test out the sample pens. I make a scribble with an orange pen. Then I grab a black one, which seems more businesslike. A better choice for Oliver. I try it out, and soon, I'm drawing one of Rory's most famous onetime games: the Barrel Dare. It happened when our neighbor gave us a cardboard barrel that special sawdust comes in for the Ganders' and donkeys' bedding. Rory rolled the barrel up the hill behind our house and climbed in, then ordered us to give the barrel a shove. In a matter of seconds, the barrel was speeding down the hill. The only sound was the steady rumble as Rory was thrown topsy-turvy inside. Gabe and I raced after her, but the barrel was too fast. It didn't stop until it hit the fence, where the Ganders were waiting excitedly and honked up a storm.

When Rory crawled out, her hair stuck straight up from the static. She wobbled a bit, then found her footing. "Who's next?" she asked.

When we didn't answer right away, Rory lifted the barrel and held it toward Gabe. "Barrel Dare!" she said.

As usual, Gabe can never say no to a dare. So back up the hill we all climbed.

"Did it hurt?" he asked before crawling in.

Rory has what my dad calls "a high tolerance for pain." So when she shrugged and said, "A bit," Gabe looked even more nervous.

"Someone's gonna end up cry-ing," I sang quietly.

"Oh, Maple, you're no fun," Rory said.

That did it. "Out of the way!" I said, pushing Gabe aside.

The barrel still smelled like sawdust inside. It smelled like a new house. "Don't push *too* hard," I said, curling into a ball.

I heard a thump, which was Rory's foot giving the barrel a kick to get me going. There was no time to be scared because all I could do was hold out my hands as I started tumbling. *Bounce, bounce, bounce* I went, and it DID hurt, and I DID want to cry! But I didn't. When the barrel hit the fence, I felt a strange sense of achievement. I'd survived!

I could see Gabe's and Rory's feet as they waited outside the opening.

"Well?" Gabe asked.

I didn't answer right away. Instead, I was very quiet. What would they do if I really got hurt? Would Rory feel bad? Would Gabe tell on her?

"Maple?" Rory's dirty face peered into the barrel. "You OK?"

I quickly closed my eyes and lay very still.

"Maple!" Rory grabbed one of my feet and started to pull.

"Don't touch her!" Gabe said. "If she broke something, you could make it worse! Go get Mom."

"No way! She'll kill me!"

"You'd deserve it if you killed Maple."

I did not like how they were talking about me as if I was dead. Shouldn't they be weeping and not worrying about getting in trouble? Those jerks. I scooted around and climbed out. When I stood up, I wobbled just like Rory had, only I fell right over.

"Got you!" I said from the ground.

"Ha!" Rory said proudly. "What'd you think?"

"That was awesome!" I lied. It's best to act tougher than you really are around Rory, or she'll treat you like a baby forever.

Just then, my mom came running out and asked us what the [bad word] we thought we were doing and put the barrel to the curb, where we put our recycling once a week.

"Earth to Maple!" Astrid says in her teacher voice, interrupting my memory. "Snap out of it!"

I look down at the paper covered in my Barrel Dare drawings.

"What's taking you so long?" Astrid asks. "It's just a pen!"

I put the black gel pen away and move down the aisle. I bet Oliver is more of a ballpoint pen kind of person anyway.

"Maple!" Katy says. "We've run out of time!"

I grab an officey-looking pen and follow them to the checkout line.

"What did you get?" I ask Astrid.

"Katy and I are going to pitch in together to get this cashbox. Isn't it cool?"

I wish they'd let me pitch in, too, so it could be from all three of us. I think she can read my thoughts because she takes the boring pen I chose and puts it on top of the box. "We'll all three give him the box and the pen, OK?"

I nod and smile. I don't know what I did to deserve friends like Astrid and Katy, but I sure feel lucky to have them.

Nine

Gabe and Rory do not stop teasing me about Oliver's party until the day finally arrives. For some reason, they think Oliver invited me because he has a crush on me, even though I explained he invited Astrid and Katy, too.

"So do you have to wear a suit to the party, or is it business casual?" Gabe asks.

"I don't know what that means," I say.

"Wear what makes you feel comfortable," my mom says.

"Don't tell her that, Mom!" Rory says. "She'll wear those gross pajama pants she loves."

I elbow Rory. I would not. I may not have any fashion sense, but I do know it would be a bad idea to wear my cat unicorn pj's to a party. Besides, they're fleece, and it's going to be a hot day. I decide to wear regular old shorts and a T-shirt and hope for the best.

"Will you be having lunch? Or a board meeting?" Rory asks just before I leave.

"Ha-ha," I say.

My dad picks up Astrid and Katy so we can all arrive at the party together. On the drive there, my dad is especially quiet. Usually, when he drives me places with my friends, he tries extra hard to be fun, playing loud music and dancing in his seat while he drives. I heard him arguing with my mom about something before we left, and I wonder if that's what put him in a sour mood.

At Oliver's house, Katy and Astrid jump out, but I hesitate and stay back.

"Are you OK, Dad?" I ask. "You seem quiet."

He doesn't answer me at first, but then he smiles in his gentle way. "Sure, Mapes. I'm OK." But he doesn't sound convincing at all.

"You have a fun time, kiddo." He puts the car in gear before I even shut my door. I quickly close it, and he rolls away.

Oliver is dressed in a bright blue suit with a matching vest. A purple tie adds a touch of flair. He looks like a very stylish tiny businessman.

If I had a themed birthday party, I'd ask everyone for art supplies. But I don't know what I would wear. What do artists wear? Probably anything they want! I could even wear my cat unicorn pajama pants, I bet.

Oliver ushers us inside and takes us to a big family room that looks out over a pretty backyard with lots of flowers and a maple tree just like mine, only his has a giant tree house in it, way up high. I had no idea Oliver had such a fancy home. Astrid nudges me and points to the tree house through the window.

"I know!" I whisper. "I wonder if we can go inside!"

It's hard to imagine Oliver in his business suit playing in a tree house. Maybe that's where he holds his board meetings. I smirk to myself, thinking Gabe would find that funny. But then I also imagine my mom telling me it's not nice to be snarky. Even so, I picture Oliver climbing the ladder in his suit, trying to lug his briefcase up with him.

We set our presents down on a polished wooden table that already has a few presents neatly wrapped and organized. I can't wait for gift-opening time to see what everyone else chose.

Once all the guests arrive, Oliver's mom leads us to the backyard, and we play a bunch of typical birthday games. Oliver takes his jacket and vest off when it gets too hot, but he refuses to remove his tie, even though his parents keep suggesting it. He's very professional, even when he's being silly.

Finally, it's time for cake and then present opening. When his dad brings out the cake, Oliver groans. "Dad! Seriously?" But he's grinning from ear to ear, so I think he actually loves it.

"That's some cake!" Katy says.

The cake is decorated to look like a file cabinet. It must have a lot of layers because I think it's about ten inches tall! The napkins are a light tan and folded in a way to make them look like file folders, each with our names written on them. The ink has run a bit on them, though. I bet his dad used a Sharpie.

Oliver looks so happy about the cake, his eyes glass over and I'm afraid he might cry. But he smiles and claps his hands together like a little kid. His dad hugs him, and his mom gets us all to sing "Happy Birthday," and then he blows out the candles.

The cake turns out to be seven layers, and each one has been dyed a different rainbow color. Not only that, but each layer has a slightly different flavor! It is by far the best cake I've ever had. I try to remember every detail because I can't wait to tell Gabe and Rory all about it.

Next is present-unwrapping time. We sit in a circle on the grass while Oliver's parents take turns bringing him a gift from the table where they were displayed earlier. I've never seen so many office supplies in one place in my life. Well, except for Staples.

He gets an electric pencil sharpener, a three-hole punch with a binder, a file box with file folders, a label maker, a fancy desk lamp, and, of course, our gift, which I personally think looks like the most fun. The final present is a book called *The Secrets of Success, Jr.* Oliver politely says thank you, but I'm sitting close enough to hear him whisper under his breath that he's already read the grown-up version.

When all the presents are opened, Oliver wants to bring his haul straight to his "office," which I can't wait to see, but his parents tell him he needs to entertain his guests and that setting up the office can come later. It turns out that Oliver's office is in the tree house, and it's top secret, so we don't get a tour, which is disappointing. I still have no idea what he actually plans to do in this office or what kind of business he has.

His VIPs, Denzel and Carmella, follow him around closely as if they are bodyguards.

"This is all a little strange," Katy whispers.

"Don't be mean," I say.

"I'm not being mean. I'm just pointing out the obvious. Don't you think it's a little strange?"

"Maybe he thinks we're a little strange," Astrid says.

"Then why would he invite us to his party?" I ask.

Astrid grins. "For the presents!"

Katy looks shocked.

"Maybe he wants to recruit us to work for him," I say. "Maybe he's trying to expand his business."

"How could it be a successful business if we still don't even know what it is?" Katy asks.

"Maybe it's top secret, and you only find out after he hires you," Astrid points out.

Before we can learn more, Astrid's dad arrives to pick us up.

Oliver seems disappointed to see us go. "Thank you for the best gift!" he says when he walks out to the driveway with us. "But don't tell the others I said that."

"That was the best birthday cake I've ever had," I tell him.

"My dad loves to bake," Oliver says. "Someday, if I have the time, I hope to help him set up his own bakery. I need to save some capital first, though."

I have no idea what that means so I just nod. "Good luck!"

To my surprise, Oliver hugs me tight.

Katy and Astrid both react by dropping their mouths open. But he rushes away before he can see.

My cheeks sting with embarrassment as I climb into Mr. Kleeber's minivan.

Please don't let them say anything. Please don't let them say anything.

"Everyone buckled in?" Mr. Kleeber asks before backing out of the driveway.

Astrid turns to me. "What was that about?" she asks.

"Yeah!" Katy says. "I was *not* expecting that!"

"Neither was I!" I say. "And how come he didn't hug you two?"

"Clearly Oliver has a crush on you," Astrid says matter-of-factly.

"No!"

"Why else would he hug only you?" Katy asks.

"How should I know? Ugh. That was weird!" I don't like how I feel. I'm positive Oliver does not have a crush on me. So why would he hug just me?

"Do you like him?" Katy asks.

I want to shout *No!* again. But I don't. I don't know how I feel about Oliver. He's nice. And he's a little strange, which is how I always think people think of *me*. I wouldn't mind being his friend. But his *girl*friend?

"No," I finally say. "He's just a friend."

"You do!" Astrid says. "You wouldn't have paused otherwise!"

Oh brother.

"I don't like him that way," I say.

Mr. Kleeber is being awfully quiet, which makes me

think he's trying to eavesdrop and get some good gossip. Well, I am not going to provide any. We drive the rest of the way to Katy's in silence.

We say our goodbyes to Katy, and then Mr. Kleeber drops me off at my place.

"Let's hang out tomorrow!" Astrid says. "We need to get the clubhouse ready for summer!"

I nod. "I'll call you!"

I hop out of the van and run to the front door. I don't know why I'm in such a hurry to get home, but for some reason, I just want to go to my room, shut the door, and think.

I sit on my bed with my sketchbook, trying to shake the feeling of Oliver hugging me. It wouldn't have been bad if he'd hugged everyone else, too. Why just me? I do want to be his friend. I wouldn't even mind going to one of his business meetings, even though I don't know what kind of business he has.

When I was little, I used to pretend I was a librarian and set up the living room with books spread out on the furniture. Then my stuffed animals would come check them out. I wonder if Oliver did that before he found real kids to join him. I imagine him sitting in his tree house at the head of a table, pretending to have a meeting with his own stuffed animals.

A knock on my door interrupts me. I close my sketchbook and push the door open a crack.

"May I help you?" I say, trying to sound like a businessperson.

"We're going on an outing!" Rory says excitedly. "Dad signed up a new client, and we're going out to celebrate."

I sit up taller and almost bump my head. That hasn't happened before. I wonder if I've grown a little. "Where to?"

"Not sure. Mom just said Dad wants to surprise us, so get ready and come downstairs."

"Can I wear what I have on?"

She looks at me. "Good enough, I bet," she says.

Gabe pokes his head in. "How was the party?" he asks. "Did you get to attend a board meeting?"

I roll my eyes. "Just move," I say, pushing the door open so I can squeeze out.

"Someone's touchy," Rory says.

I elbow her. "I'm not touchy," I say. "You just shouldn't make fun of Oliver." But I immediately feel guilty because I know that's exactly what I did with my comic. I silently make a promise to rip out that page when we get home.

Ten

My parents are already waiting in the car when we come downstairs, so the three of us squeeze into the back seat.

Since I'm the youngest and smallest, I always have to sit in the middle, which is not fun. Especially on a hot day.

"You're pressing against me too tightly," Rory says, fidgeting next to me.

Her bare arm against mine feels wet and sticky.

"I can't help it," I say. "Move over."

She tries to lean against the door, but it's no use. The three of us cannot sit back here without touching.

"We need a bigger car," Gabe says. "Either that or

Maple needs to stop growing. She's getting too big for the middle seat."

My dad leans his head out the window like he's trying Rory's dog experiment again, but really, I bet it's because he's trying to tune out the bickering.

My mom turns and gives us all her "zip it" look, which means stop fussing because it's obviously irritating Dad.

I try to squish my body tight so I'm not touching Rory or Gabe. Sometimes I wish I could be the kind of superhero who can change size. I imagine a comic of me expanding into the shape of an elephant and squeezing Rory and Gabe against their doors until they promise to do my bidding before I shrink back down to the shape of a little cat. I don't actually know what I would make them do for me, though. Maybe bring me snacks? But Rory's snacks are usually gross. Do my homework? But that would be cheating. Here I go again, overthinking.

"Where are we going, anyway?" Gabe asks.

"Someplace fun," my mom says.

"Super fun!" my dad says, bringing his head back into the car now that we're talking about something he likes.

We drive along in silence for a bit until we turn

off onto a winding dirt road that leads to a big white farmhouse on a hill. There's loud music playing. When we drive behind the house, we see all kinds of little tents set up in a field that slopes downward. At the bottom of the hill is a platform with musicians performing on it. Tons of people have spread out blankets in the tall grass to watch. Above the platform there's a big banner made from a tie-dyed sheet that says WELCOME TO ALT-WOODSTOCK!

A teenager directs us to park in another part of the field, and then we all pile out. From the way back, my mom drags out a cooler and tells us we're going to have a musical picnic.

"What's in the cooler?" Rory asks.

"Cool drinks and some apples," my mom says.

"That doesn't sound like much of a picnic," Gabe points out.

My mom sighs. "It's all I had time to throw together with such short notice." She gives my dad a look as if to blame him. He rolls his eyes and leads us toward the concert area. We stop to see what's for sale at each of the little pop-up tents. There are a few selling various kinds of homemade cookies and fudge, fresh-squeezed lemonade and cider, and another selling strawberry-rhubarb pie slices.

"We can get a treat later," my mom says. "If you're good." That's something she always told us when we were little and she didn't want us to be annoying at the grocery store. I think she kind of forgot that she doesn't need to say that anymore.

My dad leads us through patches of grass among all the picnickers until he finally finds a spot for us that's just right. We spread out two blankets while my mom unpacks the cooler and hands us our water bottles, which she's filled with the lemonade you make from powder. I can tell she put in too much because there's still a whole layer of powder at the bottom of my bottle.

"Just shake it," she says, seeing me notice.

My dad leans back on his elbows and closes his eyes, then nods his head to the music.

"Are they only going to play hippie music?" Gabe asks.

"What's hippie music?" I ask.

"This," he says, waving his hand at the stage.

"Songs from the sixties and seventies are the best," my dad says. "These songs are *meaningful*. Listen to the words, kids. They'll make you *think*. It's not like today's junk."

I try to listen to the words, but I don't really know what some of them mean. I pull my sketchbook out of my bag like I always do to pass the time.

"Is this song about socialism?" Gabe asks.

My dad grins and reaches over to squeeze Gabe's shoulder. "Right on, Gabe. Power to the people."

"Oh brother," Rory says.

My mom leans back against my dad and closes her eyes. She smiles and nods her head to the music. They look happy and peaceful. I wish they could be like this together all the time. But they hardly ever seem close anymore. Oliver's parents were like this the whole day! Everything about Oliver's house was perfect. His party, his tree house, and his parents. I bet they never fight. I can't imagine his dad yelling at his mom or storming off to be alone somewhere. They probably spend all their time together, making rainbow cakes and listening to Oliver's business plans.

I set my sketchbook down and lean back on the blanket to stare up at the sky. The clouds are white and fluffy against the blue behind them, slowly turning a pinkish orange as the sun sets. When the song ends, people clap and whistle sharply and call out titles of songs I've never heard of. People all around us sing along as the next song starts.

"Can we go get treats?" Rory asks.

My dad is too busy smiling at the stage and nodding his head to the music to answer.

"If you stick together," my mom says. She gives Gabe a few dollars and says we have to share whatever we find.

"That's not going to be enough for anything!" Rory whines.

"Why do you have to buy stuff?" my dad asks. "Why can't you be happy just sitting here listening to the music?"

"Hmph," Rory answers.

"Be inventive," my mom says, and winks at her. "It's all I have."

"C'mon," Gabe says.

Rory and I try to keep up as Gabe scurries around blankets and lounging picnickers. We check out all the food tents, but the only thing we can afford is a bag of organic popcorn. Before handing it over, the farmer tells us how she grew it herself and starts explaining the process. When she's finally done, Gabe asks if there's any melted butter to put on it, and she gets all excited and starts explaining how she made the butter, too! Rory points out that technically she didn't make it herself because a cow did all the hard work. The woman laughs and gives us an extra bag for free, which I think is pretty generous given that Rory and Gabe were being kind of annoying. We ask for an extra empty bag so we can divvy up the popcorn equally. Then we meander slowly back to our picnic spot, savoring every bite. It really does taste different from the kind you cook in the microwave.

When we find our blanket, my mom is all by herself, looking a bit sad, the way she does after she and my dad have had an argument.

"Where's Dad?" Rory asks.

"Oh . . ." She hesitates, as if she doesn't want to tell us. "He needed to use the bathroom," she says. But it seems like that's not the whole truth. I bet they did get in a fight. Again. Ugh. They were finally getting along!

"There are porta-potties down on the edge of the field." My mom points in the distance at a row of green-and-white little houses like the ones set up at fairs and big events.

"Gross," Rory says. "If I have to go, I'm definitely holding it until we get home."

I share the rest of my popcorn with my mom, and we listen to a few more songs before realizing it's been a while since my dad left.

"Maybe I should go check on him," my mom says. "It's getting dark."

"He's not a little kid," Gabe says. "Maybe he had to . . . you know. Go number two. Sometimes it takes a while."

"Especially Dad," Rory says.

My mom shoves her playfully. "Don't be rude, Rory," she says. But even though she laughs, she still seems worried.

The sky darkens and three more songs play, and my dad still hasn't returned. Lots of people have gathered their things to leave, and the spots of grass between groups have widened.

"Mom," Gabe says. "Maybe we should pack up and go look for Dad."

"You know the rules," my mom says. "We stay at our spot so we can find each other."

"Maple and I will go find him," he says. "You and Rory can stay here in case he comes back while we're gone."

"All right." My mom stands and looks all around. "We'll pack things up so we can leave as soon as you get back."

I follow Gabe across the now-almost-empty hill, back to the tents that are all closing up, over to the line of porta-potties. No one is waiting in line, and all the doors say VACANT except one.

"Must be in there," I say, pointing.

Gabe nods. We wait anxiously as it gets even more dark. Without the sun, it's getting chilly, too.

"Maybe he's sick," Gabe says.

He steps closer to the door. "Dad?" he calls. "You in there?"

There's no sound.

I start to feel scared inside. Something does not feel right. "I think he and Mom got in a fight," I say. "And Dad stormed off again."

"They were having a good time when we left them," Gabe says. "That can't be it. Mom would tell us." He knocks on the door, but no one answers.

We look around. The place is really starting to empty out.

"Maybe it's a portal," Gabe says.

"A what?"

"You know, a portal. Like the wardrobe."

"What wardrobe?"

"Don't you remember *The Lion, the Witch and the Wardrobe*? The kids climbed in and came out in Narnia!"

"Oh, that's right!" I say. "Maybe instead of a porta-potty, it's a *portal*-potty!"

Gabe cracks up. "Good one, Maple!"

"I wonder where portal-potties take you."

"Definitely not Narnia."

"Maybe Disney World?" I ask. I've always wanted to go there.

"Nahhhh, too easy."

"Maybe a world no one else knows! Like Narnia, but . . . um . . ."

"Dadlandia!" Gabe says.

"Yes! Dadlandia! Where the world is just like Dad wishes it was!"

"Hippie songs and organic snacks!"

"Free organic popcorn for everyone!"

"No GMOs!"

"One hundred percent solar powered!"

"Everyone wears tie-dye they made themselves!"

"And they all go barefoot!"

I imagine my dad wandering around happily, dancing to his favorite tunes.

"Gabe!" our mom calls.

We turn and see her and Rory rushing toward us with all the picnic gear.

"No luck?" she asks.

We shake our heads.

"There's someone in there, but they won't answer."

My mom gets her most worried look so far. She walks over to the door and knocks, but again there's no answer. She knocks harder, and an angry voice yells, "Occupied!"

It's definitely not my dad.

My mom sighs. "I guess we should go back to the car and wait there," she says.

We follow her across the grass to the parking area, where only a few cars remain. The grass is wet with the evening dew and soaks through my sneakers. It's really dark now, except for a few headlights from cars as they slowly crawl away over the bumpy ground.

"What's on our car?" Gabe asks, walking faster. "There's a big dark lump on the roof!"

My mom tries to use the flashlight on her phone, but it won't reach that far.

"It's a person!" Rory says. She takes off running.

"Wait! Rory!" my mom calls. But she starts to run, too.

Gabe and I follow.

As we get closer, we realize the lump is definitely a person.

When we get even closer and my mom's flashlight reaches the roof, we see that it's Dad. I guess he didn't make it to Dadlandia after all.

Eleven

My dad sits there, looking out at the darkened parking lot as if he's on top of a mountain enjoying the view.

As if he is in Dadlandia after all.

"Dan!" my mom says in the voice she usually saves for us kids when she's really, really mad at us. "What are you doing?"

Rory starts to climb up on the car to join him, but my mom pulls her off. "No, Rory! This isn't funny."

Usually, Rory would argue. But my mom's tone has reached the "do not mess with me" level, so Rory sulks and steps down.

"I came here for some peace and quiet," he says. It's the excuse he always gives when he wants some time away from all of us.

My mom sighs heavily and shakes her head. "Well, you found it. Hope you're happy."

"I am!" my dad says in a mean way. "You should try it sometime."

"I'd like to. But one of us has to be responsible and stay with the kids." She turns to us. "Get in the car," she says in her "don't make me ask twice" voice.

We climb in the back. The windows are unrolled a crack, though, so we can hear everything outside.

"We waited and waited for you," my mom says. "I know you're mad at me, but do the kids have to suffer? We were all really worried about you."

"Why would you be worried? It's not like this is the real Woodstock or something. It's *Alt*-Woodstock. Remember?"

"I texted you!"

"My phone's off. No one should have their phone on during a concert."

"Dan—"

The roof of the car creaks; my dad must be getting ready to come down. "This right here is why I left. You just can't stop *nagging*. NAG, NAG, NAG. All I asked was to take the family to a fun concert to celebrate finally getting a sale, and you just *had* to ruin it."

I cringe. Next to me, I feel Gabe tense. He leans back and bangs his head against the headrest. Rory turns her head to look out the window.

It gets quiet outside. I imagine my dad's words

stinging my mom right in the heart. I imagine her standing there in the dark, feeling the hurt of them and trying not to cry. That's what I would be doing, anyway.

"I'm sorry," my mom says quietly. "I didn't mean to upset you."

"We were having such a nice time, but then you had to go and complain about money. As usual. You couldn't just enjoy the music."

"I wasn't complaining! I just said I wished I had more to give the kids!"

"Same thing! Nothing is enough for you. Do you know how that kind of comment makes me feel? Like a failure."

"I didn't mean to."

"But you do it all the time!"

My mom doesn't answer. I imagine her shaking her head because I know she would never try to make my dad feel bad on purpose.

Rory, Gabe, and I stay quiet. Part of me wants to jump out of the car and tell them to stop fighting. I'm surprised Rory hasn't, to be honest. But I guess we all know it would only make things worse. My dad would probably stomp off in the dark, and then my mom would be even more worried. So we just sit and wait for the fight to be over.

"Please just get down so we can go home," my mom says.

I press my head against the back of the seat just like Gabe and close my eyes. *Maybe he should go back to Dadlandia,* I think.

After my mom and dad get in the car, we slowly drive through the bumpy field and onto the main road.

We're quiet for a while, and it feels awful. Finally, Mom peeks at us in the rearview mirror, forcing a smile in the dark. "So what was your favorite song?" she asks.

"'Satisfaction,'" my dad says, as if she was asking him. He sings a few lines from the song, about how he can't get no satisfaction.

The anger in my chest grows.

"I liked the reggae lady," Rory says. She's always quick to sense another fight and tries to change the mood. "She was cool."

"Yeah," my dad says, playing along. "She was really channeling Marley tonight, huh?"

"Who's Marley?" I ask. Maybe if we just keep the subject changed, we can pretend nothing ever happened.

My dad turns his body to face me and clutches his chest. "Who is Marley? Who raised you? How have we raised a child who doesn't know who Bob Marley is, Colleen?"

My mom shrugs. Clearly, she's still angry and not ready to pretend.

"When we get home, I'll play some songs for you," my dad says. "You're gonna love him!"

But when we get home, my mom tells us all to go to bed.

"You're no fun," my dad says.

My mom looks hurt again. Seeing her that way makes something inside me hurt, too. My dad just doesn't get that we were worried about him. He should apologize! I hug my mom good night and hope she knows that *I* think she's fun.

Up in my closet, I shut the door and watch my glow-in-the-dark stickers on the shelf above me come to life. Stars. Smiley faces. A heart. I think of my dad, sitting on top of the car without us, staring up at the sky. Did he know that we were all waiting for him? Did he wonder if we were having fun? Did he know we were worried about him? Does he really feel like a failure? I have so many questions, but I don't think I could ask any of them. One thing I know for sure, though, is that my mom doesn't try to make him feel bad on purpose. None of us do.

I switch on my little light and sit up. I grab my sketchbook and begin to draw a porta-potty. Then I sketch out some cells for a comic on the next page.

Twelve

The house is quiet when I get up the next morning. I grab my sketchbook and go downstairs as silently as I can. Sometimes it's nice to be the first one up. I like to sit in my dad's favorite chair that faces the window and look at my tree and draw. When the wind moves a branch, I pretend the tree is waving good morning to me, and I wave back.

When I was little, my mom read a book to me about a tree that loved a child and gave him everything. The tree gave and gave, and the child took and took. As the child grew, he wanted even more, so the tree kept giving parts of itself away until all that was left of it was a stump. Then the child, who had become a man, sat on it! I was so mad, I ran to my tree and promised I would never do something like that. Sometimes I even felt guilty for telling it my problems, because that feels like asking for something. But I'm really just *sharing* them, like a secret.

This morning, though, I find my dad already in the chair. He's not drinking coffee or listening to music like he usually does. He's just staring out the window. I wonder if he and my mom made up after last night's fight, or if they're still mad at each other. Part of me wants to ask. Part of me wants to tell him he wasn't very nice. But part of me thinks he already knows that.

"Morning, Dad," I say, stepping closer to his chair. He's wearing his old flannel bathrobe with the collar turned up. His hair pokes up every which way. "Would you like me to make you some coffee?"

He smiles at me. "Our way?"

"The only way," I reply.

Last year, Dad taught me how to make coffee on Mother's Day, when I suggested we make breakfast for Mom and bring her breakfast in bed, like on Mother's Day ads. Personally, I think it's gross to eat food in bed. But coffee seems OK. My dad has a special way of making coffee called the pour-over method. He's against coffeemakers and thinks you should make it the "real" way.

"That would be nice, honey."

"I can make some for Mom, too. Is she up yet?"

"Not yet. Didn't you notice how peaceful it is?" He chuckles a little.

"That's not very nice, Dad!"

"Oh, come on. I'm only kidding."

"It's not funny."

"What's gotten into you, Maple, sheesh. You're as serious as your mother."

I'm so mad, I nearly stomp off. But instead, I take a deep breath. "I happen to like Mom, so I'll take that as a compliment," I say.

I bet Astrid would call my behavior "passive-aggressive," and she would probably be right.

My dad sighs, as if I'm tiring him out. "I'm sorry, Mapes. You're right. That wasn't a nice thing to say. I didn't mean it."

I look in his eyes, and it does seem like he feels bad. In fact, he looks sad. Really sad. "OK," I say. "I'll still make your coffee."

I go to the kitchen and fill the teakettle with water. While I wait for it to heat, I grind a scoop of coffee beans for exactly the time it takes to sing the alphabet, then put the beans in their special filter. I like the smell of the freshly ground coffee—which is *not* the same as coffee breath—but I have to be careful sniffing because one time I put my nose too close when I sniffed, and some grinds went right up it and made me sneeze about a million times.

I hum a song I liked from the concert last night about three little birds while I wait for the water to get hot enough. Then, when everything's ready, I carefully carry Dad's favorite mug to him. Only, when I come around the corner, his chair is empty.

"Dad?" I say.

I put the hot mug on a coaster sitting on the side table next to his chair.

Through the window, the tree is still waving. I peer out to see if my dad is outside, but the yard is empty.

"Dad?" I say louder.

Maybe he went to the bathroom.

But when I check, the door is open and he's not there, either.

Maybe our bathroom is a portal-potty, too.

I wander all through the downstairs and don't see him anywhere.

Maybe he went back to bed.

I sit in the chair, his coffee getting cold in the mug, and watch my tree. It waves its branches gently at me. I think about my dad, sitting on top of our car last night, without a care. Not a care in the whole wide world. Not even for us.

The smell of his coffee doesn't smell good anymore.

I hate it. He knew I was making him a mug. Why did he go off and let it go to waste?

When my mom comes down, she looks at the mug of coffee. "You should not be drinking that," she tells me, all serious.

"It's not mine. I made it for Dad."

"Oh. Where is he?"

"I thought he went back to bed."

She makes her concerned face. "No, he got up ages ago."

"He was here when I came down, so I offered to make him coffee, but when I came back to give it to him, he was gone." I decide to leave out the part about his mean comment and my snarky reply. Maybe he left because I annoyed him.

I follow my mom to the front door.

"The car's gone," she says. "Where'd I leave my phone?"

I shrug.

I stand in the open doorway as she goes back inside to see if he texted her. The air is warm and calm. I walk outside and sit on the front step, where the sun is shining. I close my eyes and feel the sun on my face. Usually, I like how this feels, but this time all I feel is frustration about my dad. My parents always make us tell them where we're going when we leave the house, even if it's just to play in the backyard. So how come he doesn't have to follow the rules? Now I understand the reason for them better. It helps to know where the people you love are. So you don't worry.

"No message," my mom says from behind me. She steps down and sits next to me, so close our arms touch. She sets her phone down and sighs.

"Maybe he went to get doughnuts," I say.

"Maybe," she says, like she doubts it.

"Mom," I say.

But before I can go on, she puts her arm around me and squeezes me close. "Guess he just needed some Space Time," she says. "Do you think he'd mind if I heated up the coffee you made for him? It would be a shame to waste it."

"In the microwave?" My dad always lectures us about how you're not supposed to heat water for tea or coffee in the microwave, but I never really understood why.

"It can be our secret," my mom says. She gives me another squeeze, then stands up and stretches in some sort of yoga pose that I hope none of the neighbors see.

"Join me?" she asks. "We can make some toast or something."

I guess that means she definitely doesn't think Dad

is out getting doughnuts. I want to hold out hope, though.

"I'm not hungry yet," I say.

She pauses, as if she wants to say more. I want to say more, too. I want to ask her what's going on with her and my dad. Why is he always so mad at her? Do they still love each other? Are they going to get a divorce, like Katy's parents did? But part of me isn't sure I want to know the answer. Or maybe part of me already does know the answer and just doesn't want to hear it out loud. So I stay quiet, and my mom does, too. Instead, she pats the top of my head before leaving me on the steps and goes inside.

Thirteen

I'm still sitting on the front steps when I hear Astrid calling to me from the street.

"Hey, Maple!" she says, running up the driveway. She's out of breath when she gets to me, as if she ran all the way to my house.

"You ready to start planning?" She slides her backpack off her shoulders and sits down next to me.

"Planning what?" I ask.

"My clubhouse updates and your tree fort plan!" she says. "Remember?"

"Oh," I say, remembering I told her we'd meet up today. "I said I'd call first."

Astrid shrugs. "I was bored, so I decided to just come over." She unzips her bag and takes out a brand-new spiral notebook and pencil.

"When did you have time to get that?" I ask.

"Oh, you know my mom. She always has way too many backup school supplies. It's almost the end of the year, so I'm pretty sure no one will need it at this point."

Astrid's mom is a teacher at another school and buys supplies for kids who can't afford them. "Let's work on your clubhouse improvements first," I say.

"Do you want to go get your sketchbook?"

I look at the thin-lined paper and shrug. Usually, I would say yes and run in to get my sketchbook and Sharpie. But for some reason, I don't feel like drawing or looking at my plans for my own tree fort that was supposed to be started last summer.

"Here, you draw," Astrid says. "You're so much better than me."

I take the notebook and pencil.

"Start with what we have so far," she says. "And then we can go from there."

I sketch out her clubhouse in the shade of a tree behind her house.

"What should we add to keep the ABC's out?" Astrid asks, looking over my shoulder. "I'm thinking a padlock, for extra security."

"Your door already locks," I say.

"Yeah, but only once you're inside. A padlock would mean we could lock it up while we're not there."

"Good idea," I say. "You could wear the key to the lock on a string around your neck so you won't lose it and no one can ever take it!"

"Yeah!" she says. "They had some of those for sale at Staples."

I draw a little lock on the door handle.

"What else?" I ask. As I wait for her to answer, I draw Astrid's dog, Jud, looking out the window of the clubhouse.

"I know!" Astrid says when I finish. "We could make a sign that says 'Members Only.' That way, the ABC's can't say they didn't know they were trespassing. Remember that time they broke in before and then said they were just visiting?"

"Good thinking!" I say. I make a little rectangle on the door, then pass the notebook and pencil back to her. "You should probably write it since we know I'm not the world's best speller."

Astrid carefully writes out the letters so they fit in my small sign space.

"That should do it," she says.

"Anything else?" I ask. "Your clubhouse really is already pretty nice."

"But nothing like Oliver's," Astrid says.

Ugh. Why did she have to bring him up?

"Well, his is almost too nice," I say. "Know what I mean?"

"Yes! I do! Like, you probably have to take your shoes off to go in there, it's so perfect and tidy."

"There's probably hand sanitizer right inside the door!" I add.

Astrid snickers, then stops. "That's not nice of us to say."

I feel a pang of guilt. "You're right. Sorry."

"It's OK," she says. "I won't tell anyone."

"Me either."

I take the notebook back and add some details to the background so it looks more and more like Astrid's yard. Just as I finish, I see our car slow down and turn into the driveway.

Dad!

I jump up and the notebook falls to the ground. "Sorry!" I say. But I run over to the car without even picking it up.

"You're back!" I say through my dad's open window.

"Of course I'm back," he says. "And . . . look what I brought!" He reaches over to the passenger seat and pats a big box of doughnuts from our favorite bakery.

"Yay!" I say. "My dad got us doughnuts!" I call over

to Astrid. I feel so relieved that he left to do something nice after all, and not because of our argument. I can't stop smiling.

"Is anyone else up yet?" Dad asks.

"Mom," I say. "I gave her your coffee."

His happy face sags a little. "What time is it?" he asks.

"How should I know? Where's your phone?"

"Right." He gets out of the car and reaches in his pajama pants pocket.

"Dad! You wore your pj's out in public?"

He grins. "Everyone does it these days! Besides, I used the drive-through! Don't worry, no one saw me."

Just then my mom comes out of the house. "You're back!" she says. She looks relieved, happy, and angry all at once. "Why didn't you tell me you were going out?"

"Can I take the doughnuts in?" I interrupt, before they can start arguing. I run around the car without waiting for an answer.

"C'mon!" I say to Astrid. "Let's grab the best ones before Gabe and Rory wake up!"

We race inside with the box, leaving my mom and dad in the driveway. I turn back once and see my dad lean against the car while my mom waves her hands around the way she does when she's yelling at us kids. I can already imagine him saying all the things he does when she gets angry like this. *You're so uptight. You worry too much. Calm down for once. Lower your voice, for God's sake.*

I wish she wouldn't get so mad at him. He wasn't gone that long. But the more I think about it, the more I realize he was gone awhile. At least way longer than it takes to get doughnuts.

So . . . where else was he? Did he take a side trip to Dadlandia? Maybe he needed some time and space to cool off after all.

"Maple!" Astrid says. "Which kind is your favorite?"

I turn to the box of doughnuts. Two are already missing, which means my dad must have scarfed them down on his drive home. Or maybe he ate them in the parking lot by himself, instead of back here with us. Just thinking about it makes me sad again. Sad and worried and annoyed all at once. It's too many feelings to have all at the same time, and it makes my stomach hurt. It makes me wonder if this is how my mom feels, too.

"I don't know," I tell Astrid. I grab a jelly one with pink frosting on top, and she gets a Boston cream. Usually I would have inspected each one before making a choice, deciding which is the biggest and has the best filling. But my heart isn't in it.

Astrid takes a big bite of hers, and some cream squirts out and drips onto her shirt. She lifts her shirt up and licks it off, laughing. "I am not letting one drop go to waste!" she says. "My parents never get doughnuts!"

I smile, trying to shove my feelings away somewhere. "Are you OK?" Astrid asks. "You seem a little upset."

Instead of answering, I take a giant bite of my own doughnut. But all the sweetness in the world can't make this bitter feeling go away.

Fourteen

I can't believe you two ate all the good doughnuts before we came downstairs," Rory says, picking each one up to inspect which kind it is.

"You snooze, you lose," I tell her.

Gabe slides the box out of her reach. "Get your grubby hands off those! You are so disgusting!"

"My hands are clean! I just woke up!" Rory holds out her hands. There are powdered-sugar smudges and cinnamon-sugar marks all over the tips of her fingers.

"You slept all night with your gross hands in your gross sheets and then probably peed and didn't wash your hands after, and now you are touching every single doughnut!"

"I didn't pee yet!" Rory argues. "So there was no reason to wash my hands. And why are you so weird about clean hands all of a sudden?"

"Because I care about germs! And I don't want your gross ones!"

"Let's go outside," I say to Astrid. "This isn't going to end well."

We go out to the tire swing and climb on either side so the rope is between us. We swing gently without needing to talk, our knees pressing against each other.

When I was younger, I could fit inside the tire and adjust myself just so, as if I was lying in a hammock. One time I came out here and climbed into the swing after Gabe and Rory had been mean to me. I tired myself out telling my tree all the things they did and how it made me feel. So much so that I fell sound asleep! When Rory found me, she thought it would be funny to quietly start pushing me higher and higher. When I woke up, I was soaring in the tire so high, I fell right out! I landed with a thud and couldn't breathe. Rory thought I was dead. When I came to, she felt so guilty, she told me to swing her as hard as I could and try to knock her out to make us even. But before I could, my mom spotted us through the window and sang-yelled at us through the screen door, "Someone's gonna end up cry-ing!"

But she was too late. I already was.

• • •

"I'm glad I'm an only child," Astrid says as we listen to things heat up inside.

I hear Rory call for my mom, and then my dad's raised voice, which almost never happens. My mom is usually the one to step in and stop our fights. My dad is the peacemaker who helps us make up after. He really hates it when we don't get along and usually leaves the room until things settle down. That's the kind of thing my parents argue about, too. My mom says it's unfair that she always has to be the "bad guy." And then my dad says, "No one's making you be the bad guy. Just let them work it out themselves." And then she says, "You're the one who gets upset when they fight. I'm just trying to keep you from getting upset." And then he says something like, "I never asked you for any favors." And then she makes a hurt face, and my dad walks off, which is how he avoids conflict, I guess. At least, that's how Rory explains it. She says some people want the last word, so they keep arguing, and some people will avoid conflict at all costs, so they walk away. Rory is definitely a keep-arguing type. So is Gabe. I guess I am, too, if I think I'm in the right. But not my dad. He would rather stomp off and disappear so no one sees him get angry.

When things finally quiet down inside the house, I try to imagine what it would be like to be an only child, like Astrid. It would be a lot quieter, that's for sure. But I bet it would also be boring.

"Do you get lonely sometimes?" I ask Astrid. "Not having someone to talk to or play with whenever you want?"

"That's what Jud is for," Astrid says.

"Dogs are nice," I say. "But they aren't the same as a brother or sister."

"Jud is," Astrid says. "In fact, he's better."

"Because he can't talk?" I joke.

Astrid smirks. "No, because he doesn't like to fight. He always wants to play, and he always knows when I'm feeling sad."

"That sounds nice," I say.

We sway back and forth, and I think of Jud, and how much fun it is to play with him when I go to Astrid's house.

"Maybe a dog *would* be better than a sibling," I say, imagining Gabe and Rory as dogs instead of humans. I'd throw them sticks to fetch, and they'd wag their tails happily and do anything I asked. And we could go for long walks through the neighborhood, like Astrid and Jud do. I picture putting Dog-Gabe and Dog-

Rory on leashes and leading them around with me. But then—

"Ack!" I say. "I know one way dogs are *not* like siblings!"

"How?" Astrid says, doubt in her voice.

"I don't have to pick up their poop in a special bag when we go for walks!"

Astrid starts to giggle, then she laughs so hard, she almost falls off the swing.

"Maple, sometimes you are so gross!" she says.

"Blame it on Gabe and Rory," I tell her. "They taught me everything I know."

The screen door slams, and my dad wanders out to the backyard. He looks surprised when he sees us on the swing.

"Oh! Hi, girls. What are you doing out here?"

"Swinging!" I say.

He nods. "Is that what that is?"

"Very funny, Dad. Astrid and I have been talking about the tree fort." I look above us at the three big branches I think would be the perfect place to secure the floor.

"Tree fort?"

"Yes! The one we're going to make together this summer."

"You girls are going to make a tree fort? Good for you!"

"No, Dad. *You're* going to make it. With my help, of course. Remember? You promised? We were going to do it last summer, but you got too busy."

He scratches his head and looks up at the branches. "I did?"

"Yes, Dad." I hate it when he gets like this, and I can't tell if he's joking or just being weird and forgetful. I don't see how he could forget something that's so important to me. He already bought the supplies! They're just sitting all piled up next to the garage.

"I'm just messing with you, Mapes," he says. "Of course I remember. Yeah, we'll build a tree fort. The best in the neighborhood!"

"This summer!" I say. "Right?"

"This summer," he says. "Right."

"You should come see my clubhouse for ideas," Astrid tells him. "We think you could make Maple's even better! With a rope ladder you can pull up behind you so no intruders can come in."

He smiles. "That's a good idea!" He gives us a little push on the swing, then turns to go back inside. It makes me wonder why he came out here in the first place. Probably to get some space.

"Your dad is so nice," Astrid says.

That reminds me that I didn't thank him for the doughnuts.

"Dad!" I call after him.

He stops partway up the steps and turns to us, lifting his hand to his forehead to block the sun shining on his face.

"Thanks for the treats!" I call to him.

"Yes!" Astrid calls. "Thank you, Dan!" Astrid is my only friend who calls my parents by their first names. My parents don't mind, but Katy's dad thinks it's disrespectful. I only know this because I overheard my mom and Mr. Willis discussing it one time.

My dad waves and goes back inside.

"Let's go to my house," Astrid says. "All this talk about dogs made me miss Jud."

"OK," I say. "Let me go tell my parents."

Astrid walks around the house to wait out front while I run inside. The empty doughnut box sits on the dining room table, but I don't see anyone else around. "Hello?"

"In here!" my mom calls from the kitchen.

"Where did everyone go?" I ask when I find her standing in front of the open refrigerator.

"Gabe is taking a shower, and Rory is sulking because of their fight. I don't know where Dad is, as usual."

"What are you doing?" I ask to change the subject.

She frowns and closes the door. "Oh, just trying to figure out what to make for dinner later."

"Is it OK if I go over to Astrid's? She misses her dog."

She smiles at me. "That's sweet," she says.

"Astrid thinks Jud is better than having a brother or sister."

"Oh yeah?"

I nod.

"Why's that?"

"Because he's always nice to her."

"Hmm," my mom says. "What do you think of that?"

"I mean, she has a point. But Gabe, Rory, and I don't *always* fight. And we have a lot of fun when we get along. I think I still prefer them to a dog. But . . . could we get a dog? We could get the kind that doesn't cause allergies!"

"I think you three are enough to handle for now," my mom says. "Maybe someday."

I know very well that "maybe someday" always means "not very likely."

"I bet you'd like to have a dog, Mom. Astrid says they are very loving."

My mom gives me a strange look. "You think I need more love?"

I walk over to her and give her a big hug. "Only sometimes," I say. "I'm sorry when we forget to hug you."

She squeezes me back and hugs extra hard. "Oh, honey. I get enough."

"I still think you'd like a dog. Dogs come when you call. They always want to be by your side, and they always want to give you love. Kind of like me!" I pant at her like I think a dog would.

She gives me a little shove. "Get outta here, silly. Have fun at Astrid's."

"OK."

As Astrid and I walk through the neighborhood, I think about what my mom said and about how she didn't know where my dad was. *As usual.* I hope they aren't in another fight. It seems like they are always arguing or acting mad at each other for no reason. Only, I suppose my mom often *does* have a reason to be frustrated. I just wish . . . I don't know what I wish. I guess I just wish she wouldn't get so upset with him. And I wish he wouldn't be, well, so upsetting in the first place.

Fifteen

Jud comes charging toward me and Astrid as soon as we step onto her driveway. He has a special collar that keeps him from going off their property. He wags his tail so hard, his whole bum shakes, and it looks like he's doing a little dance.

"See?" Astrid says, all serious. "I bet Gabe and Rory never looked this happy to see *you*."

She has a point. I let Jud lick my face, even though it's kind of yucky and his breath smells strange. "They also don't try to lick me!" I say, wiping his slobber off me.

"Touché," Astrid says.

"Two-what?"

"It's what you say when someone makes a good point."

"Oh."

I follow Astrid and Jud to the clubhouse out back.

"It's nice in here," I say, sitting at the tiny table we made from a cardboard box. There are three crates for chairs—one for me, one for Astrid, and one for Katy.

"I bet it's not as nice as Oliver's tree house, though," Astrid says.

"What do you think it looks like inside?"

"I bet it's like a real house. With a little bed and a table or something. And office stuff, of course. Oliver has the best of everything."

"Yeah," I agree. "Must be nice."

"I guess," Astrid says, sitting next to me. "But if you had everything you wanted, it might be kind of strange. Like, what would you wish for?"

"World peace?"

She smiles. "You know what I mean. I just think it would be strange not to long for something."

"What do you long for?" I ask.

Jud walks in a circle and then sits at our feet and pants.

"Well, sometimes I would like another dog so Jud wouldn't be lonely while I'm at school. Or a special padlock for this door, like we talked about. Or there's this pair of sneakers I like, but my mom says they are way too expensive. Stuff like that."

I nod. Most of the time I get hand-me-downs from Gabe and Rory, so I know what it's like to want something new, that no one else has worn yet. In fact, the jeans I'm wearing are so worn, the knees are *almost* see-through. Some of my clothes have been through both Rory and Gabe before they got to me. Sometimes I like that. I remember when they wore them and think about all the adventures they've seen. But sometimes, I just want something to feel like mine. Like my sketchbook.

"My sketchbook!" I say, realizing I forgot it at home.

"What about it?" Astrid says.

I feel panic rising in my chest. Where did I leave it? The kitchen counter! Who might see it? Would they open it without my permission?

"I left it at home."

"So?"

"What if someone looks in it?"

"It's just drawings, right?"

Just drawings? Ugh.

"They're private," I say. "It's like . . . a diary!"

"Oh. Sorry. Do you want to go home?"

I think about it. My family knows how important my book is to me. And how private. They wouldn't look. Would they?

No.

No, they would never.

Would they?

I shake my head. "No, it should be OK." But I still feel uneasy.

Something lands on the roof of the clubhouse and Jud growls.

"What was that?" I ask.

"An acorn?" Astrid asks.

Jud jumps to his feet and sticks his big head out the window.

Another sound comes from the roof. Like a light *plunk*.

Jud barks.

Astrid brings her finger to her lips and motions to the window. She crawls toward it and peeks outside, then quickly drops her head below the sill. "It's the ABC's! We're under attack!"

She motions to the white bucket in the corner full of acorns we've collected for just such an emergency. I nod and crawl toward it, carefully sliding it over so we can both take a handful.

"You better go away!" Astrid calls.

Jud barks again.

"Hello-ooo!" a voice says from outside the door. "Anybody home?"

"I'll let Jud out and then you'll be sorry!" Astrid says.

"Juddy boy, come here!" one of them calls sweetly. "Wanna cookie?"

Jud leaps up and squeezes through the window. The sound of giggles erupts outside the door.

"Awww, good boy. Here you go!"

"That darn dog!" Astrid says. "Jud, you traitor! You jerks better not hurt my dog!"

"We just came over to see if you wanted to hang out!" one of the ABC's says. "You don't have to be such snobs!"

"Snobs?" Astrid says. "We are not snobs!"

"Well, we are not dog hurters!" one of them says.

"Now what?" I whisper to Astrid.

We both sit still, our backs leaning against the door.

"Let me think," Astrid whispers back.

"What's so special about that clubhouse, anyway?" an ABC asks. "Aren't you too old for playing house?"

"That does it!" Astrid jumps up and motions for me to move aside. She swings open the door and puts her hands on her hips. "We are not playing house!"

I get up and stand behind her. "Yeah!"

Someone tosses an acorn, and it lands at Astrid's feet. Jud runs over to sniff it.

"Then what *are* you doing in there?" one of them asks.

"None of your business!" Astrid says.

"Astwid?" a tiny voice says.

Astrid steps out of the house to see who spoke, and I follow.

Little Dora pokes her head around one of her brothers. I should know who is who, but I don't.

"Hello, hoe-sy!" she says.

"Hello who?" Astrid asks.

"She said 'horsey,'" an ABC says. "She struggles with pronouncing her *r*'s."

"Oh!" Astrid says. "Jud's not a horse."

Dora giggles. "I know that. He just looks like one!"

I giggle, too. Jud *is* kind of tall. Especially next to Dora.

"It's not funny!" an ABC says. "Don't make fun of our sister!"

Dora looks like she's going to cry.

"No, no!" I say. "I wasn't laughing at her. I was laughing because she's right! Horsey is a great name. If he didn't already have one, I mean."

Dora takes a few steps closer to Jud. He sniffs her face, then licks her cheek.

"I've always wondered what kind of dog he is," an ABC says.

"He's a mutt," Astrid says. "But the vet thinks he has mastiff in him. That's a big-dog breed."

"Can I ride him?" Dora asks.

"No, that would hurt his back."

"We can't have any pets because our mom is allergic to everything," another ABC says.

Dora sniffs.

"Are you allergic, too?" I ask her.

She shakes her head, then puts both arms around Jud to hug him.

I've never seen the ABC's seem so . . . regular. I think back to all our encounters with them. I guess it has been a while since they did something bad. Maybe the bus incident really was just an accidental trip? I feel guilty that I don't know who is who. I wonder if they share all the same clothes or if they get to have their own. It must be interesting to look the same as two other people. I have a million questions for them, but I get the sense that all my questions would be considered rude.

"So," Astrid says. "How come you guys are being nice to us all of a sudden?"

"What do you mean?" one of them asks.

"Well, you used to call us names and break into my clubhouse," Astrid says. "What gives?"

"We haven't done that in ages," one of them says.

"Yeah, that was little-kid stuff," another says.

"Why did you change?" I ask.

"Uh, we grew up?" the one wearing a plain white T-shirt says.

"Oh."

"So, not to be rude," Astrid says.

"Uh-oh, she's about to be rude," the ABC in the gray shirt with a blue stripe says.

"I know what your names are," she continues. "But I can't tell you apart."

"Seriously?" white shirt asks.

"You do kind of look alike," I point out.

"That's fair," gray shirt says. "I'm Adam. And I keep telling these two to stop getting the same haircut as me so we can look different, but they refuse."

He has short hair on the sides and slightly long on the top, which falls over his eyes. All three of them have the same style, and they are always flipping their heads to the right to swing their bangs out of the way.

"I'm Bryce," the white-shirted one says.

"So you're Charlie," Astrid says. "I like your shirt."

Charlie's shirt is purple, which is Astrid's favorite color. He blushes when she says it, and Adam elbows him to tease him.

"How do *you* tell your brothers apart?" Astrid asks Dora.

Dora makes a silly face and shrugs. "I just do!"

"So if they went in the clubhouse and changed shirts and came back out, you could still tell who's who?" I ask.

"Of course!"

"But we're not doing that," Bryce says. "Because we aren't a game."

"That's fair," Astrid says, smiling.

"So," Charlie says. "Do you guys want to hang out?"

I can't help feeling a little nervous. These are the ABC's! What if they're just pretending to be nice so they can play a prank on us?

"That depends on what you want to do," Astrid says.

"Let's put on a circus with your dog!" Dora says. "We can teach him tricks!"

"Uh, no," Astrid says. "Sorry, but he isn't a game, either."

"Can we see your clubhouse?" Bryce asks.

Astrid looks over at me. The clubhouse? Our secret hideout? The place we were going to make a special sign for? And get a padlock for?

I shake my head ever so slightly.

"See?" Adam says. "I told you they wouldn't want to. They're just like that snob Oliver."

"Oliver is not a snob," Astrid says.

"I bet *you* got invited to his party," Bryce says.

All three of them look a little sad about that.

"We did," Astrid admits. "But I promise, Oliver isn't a snob."

"Maybe he was only allowed to invite a certain number of people," I say, trying to make them feel better.

Charlie shrugs. "Maybe."

"I'm sorry," Astrid says. "But you're going to have to earn our trust."

"Suit yourself," Adam says. "C'mon, guys. We're not wanted."

The boys turn to leave, but Dora clings to Jud again, hugging him tight.

"Don't squeeze too hard, you'll hurt him!" Astrid says.

Dora lets go and frowns. "You two aren't nice."

Oof. I was not expecting her to say that. Is she right?

"Sorry," Astrid says. "But your brothers haven't always been nice to us."

The boys are already walking down the driveway. Dora sticks her tongue out at us and runs to catch up.

Astrid and I stand there and watch her go. Jud wags his tail kind of slowly, as if he's disappointed to see them leave.

I follow Astrid and Jud back into the clubhouse and shut the door.

"Well," Astrid says, picking up an acorn off the floor. "I sure wasn't expecting that."

"Me neither."

"Too bad they left in such a huff."

"How can they blame us for not trusting them yet?" I ask. "It's not like they've ever been nice to us before. Remember when we were in kindergarten and they peed in the bushes at my house?"

"Oh my gosh, I forgot all about that!"

"Rory was so mad. She called them the PeeBodies for a whole year!"

Astrid giggles. "PeeBodies. That was a good one. Do you really think they've changed?"

"I'm not sure," I tell her. "It seems so?"

Jud rolls over, and Astrid leans forward to scratch his belly. She finds just the right place to make his back paw pedal the air really fast.

"It's so weird how dogs do that," I say.

Astrid seems lost in thought.

"I should probably go home," I tell her. I don't explain that I still feel uneasy not having my sketchbook with me, like I'm missing part of myself. Something important.

"Are you sure? I could help you study for the math quiz or something."

"I don't need help studying."

"But . . . you haven't aced it yet. And time is running out."

"It's not because I don't know the answers!"

"OK, don't get mad," Astrid says. "I was just trying

to help. Maybe if you practice with a timer, you would get used to it and not let Ms. Kent's bother you so much."

"No timers! I hate them!"

"Yeesh, fine. Sorry."

Ugh. I didn't mean to make her feel bad.

"Sorry," I say. "I just don't like them. I don't want to think about it."

I get up to go, having made things worse.

"So are we going to trust the ABC's—I mean Adam, Bryce, and Charlie—or not?" Astrid asks.

"We don't have to decide today. Let's see how they treat us at school next week."

I give Jud a pet before I step outside. "Bye," I say.

"See you at school."

I walk back home alone, slowly, thinking about Adam, Bryce, and Charlie. About what it's like living with a brother and sister instead of a dog. About hand-me-downs and clubhouses. And whether people can really change.

Astrid says she's not lonely at all, not having any siblings. I guess if you've never had one, you wouldn't know what you're missing. Sometimes, I get so mad at Gabe and Rory, I wish I was an only child. But that feeling never lasts. Whenever I'm apart from them for long, I start to miss them. Or when I do something really fun, I want to tell them about it. Like today, when Dora thought Jud was a horse. And how Adam, Bryce, and Charlie were suddenly so nice.

I start walking a little faster, eager to get home to tell them all about it. Pretty soon, instead of moping as I walk down the street, I'm practically skipping.

Sixteen

As soon as I get home, I run up the driveway and into the house. I rush into the kitchen to find my sketchbook, but it's gone.

My sketchbook is gone.

Which means someone touched it.

Which means someone could have looked inside!

Which means someone could have read my PRIVATE comics!

I feel my heart start to beat inside my chest. Not beat. Thump. Pound.

My mom and dad are talking in the dining room, so I race over to them.

"Who took my sketchbook!" I demand.

They both turn, startled by the sound of my voice. When my mom faces me, I see that she's crying. She quickly wipes her face.

"Oh, hi, honey," she says. "No one took your sketchbook. I put it in your room for safekeeping."

"Did you read it?" I ask, still not really registering that she's crying, or why.

"Of course not!" she says. She wipes her face again.

"Promise!" I yell.

"Maple. Calm down," my dad says. "What's gotten into you?"

"My sketchbook is private!" I say. "No one is supposed to touch it. Ever!"

"Stop yelling, Maple. You're being ridiculous," he says.

Hot prickles of rage heat up my face. "It is not ridiculous! How could you even say that?"

"Honey," my mom says. "It's OK. I promise you I did not look at your sketchbook. I put it in your room because I know it's private and you wouldn't want it lying around."

I take some deep breaths and let her words sink in. That's when I also let it sink in that she's been crying.

"Wait a minute," I say. "What's going on here? Why are you crying?"

She shakes her head. "It's nothing, hon. Dad and I were just having a talk about some things."

"What kind of things?"

She smiles and wipes her face again. "Never mind that. Don't worry."

"Are you having a fight?" I ask.

My mom turns away from me, as if she doesn't want me to see that she's started crying again or something.

"Just give us a minute," my dad says.

"But—"

"Out!" my dad interrupts.

"Dan!" my mom kind of whimpers. "Please don't yell."

He slams his hand down on the table, and my mom and I jump at the same time.

My dad swears. "You're the one who's always saying I shouldn't walk away when I get angry, Colleen! Is this better?"

My mom looks at me and then at my dad. More tears escape, and she tries to wipe them away again. "Not in front of the kids," she says quietly.

"Which is why I told her to get out!" my dad says, turning to me.

I take a step back. My chest hurts all over again. My heart aches as if it's telling me something terrible is about to happen, like when I'm scared watching a movie, or when I wake up from a nightmare.

"Dan," my mom tries again.

But I don't want to make him angrier. I don't want to see or hear what happens next. I can't!

I turn and run upstairs to get my sketchbook, then hurry outside. I run to my tree and hug it, pressing my forehead against the trunk. I wish it could hug me back. I wish it could tell me things will be OK.

"Please, please, make everything better," I cry. I turn my face and hold my cheek against the tree's cool, rough bark and squeeze harder, dropping my sketchbook to the ground. Above me, the branches rustle in a tiny breeze, as if the tree is whispering, *Hush*. I close my eyes and let my tears drip down my face.

"Maple!" Rory calls.

I look in the direction of her voice and see her with Gabe, down by the fence, watching the Ganders. I pick up my sketchbook and run to them.

The Ganders squawk at me when I get close.

"Mom and Dad are having a terrible fight," I say. "Mom was crying!"

"We know," Rory says. She dangles a stick over the fence. The Ganders peck at it and honk quietly.

"We should do something!" I say.

Gabe turns to me and sees my wet face. "Quit crying, Maple. All parents fight. You know that. At least they're talking and Dad didn't take off for once. Maybe this is a good thing."

"It didn't sound good," I say. "Dad was being extra mean."

"Or you were being extra sensitive," Rory says.

"I was not!"

She sighs. "OK, OK, sheesh. You know Mom and Dad. They love each other! They'll make up. They always do."

I climb onto the fence and squeeze between them.

Gabe nudges his leg against mine. "Try not to worry so much."

We don't talk for a long time, which is not like us at all. I think it's because they're worried, too, even if they don't want to admit it. So we just sit quietly together, our worry keeping us there on the fence. Waiting.

After a while, Rory drops the stick. Salt picks it up in his beak and waddles away from us. Pepper follows him, reaching out every so often to try to take the stick away, but Salt won't let him.

"Do you think the geese are like us?" Rory asks.

Gabe shifts on the fence. "What do you mean?"

"Always fighting over stuff, but also getting together

when things get tough, or when they have to protect their territory."

"We aren't *always* fighting over stuff," Gabe says.

"You know what I mean."

I think about how Rory and Gabe stand up for me sometimes, and how they are kind of like Salt and Pepper, too.

"I think Gabe is like Pepper, and Rory is like Salt," I say.

Rory jumps down from the fence. "I don't know if that's a compliment."

"It's just an observation," I say, feeling a bit like Astrid for using a big word.

Gabe and I jump down, too. The three of us stand at the fence and watch the Ganders chase each other. It seems like they're playing, not fighting.

"Maybe you should have a rematch on your race," I say. "I da—"

"Do *not* dare me," Rory interrupts. "I'm never doing that again." She rubs her bum as if remembering getting goosed there.

I give my sketchbook a squeeze, thinking about the funny comic I made.

"Well, what *do* you want to do?" I ask. "We can't go inside."

"Swing Dare?" Rory asks.

"Uh . . ." I say. The Swing Dare is another one of Rory's inventions that almost always ends up with someone crying.

A smirk forms on Gabe's face. "Race you!"

Rory takes off toward the tire swing before we can answer.

"Cheater!" I say as I run after her.

Gabe passes me and catches up to Rory just before she touches the tire. "Ha!" he says, pushing her aside. "I get to go first!"

Seventeen

"Take your marks," Gabe says, pulling the tire swing toward him.

I carefully set my sketchbook against the tree on the opposite side of the swing. "Someone's gonna end up cry-ing," I sing under my breath. "But it won't be me!"

Swing Dare is a game that Rory will definitely not be allowed to teach kids if she becomes a gym teacher.

Rory and I plant our feet in the grass not far from Gabe. He pulls the tire up above his head, then hurls it toward us. The rule is you cannot move your feet. You either have to brace yourself for impact, dip your body low enough so the tire swings over you, or lean to the side to avoid getting hit. If you manage to catch the tire, then you get to hurl it at someone else. If you jump out of the way and move your feet, you lose. BUT, if you catch the swing and jump on it, as long as you don't touch the ground and can land back where you were, you're safe. Last one standing wins.

The tire comes careening toward me, but I manage to lean out of the way just in time. It swings back to Gabe, and he grabs it again. This time, he aims for Rory, who dives through the hole and dangles there, hands flailing on one side, legs wriggling on the other. She shrieks triumphantly as she sails toward Gabe, who crouches down to avoid her, but she easily knocks him over.

"Ow!" he says when he hits the ground.

"You're out!" Rory yells.

"My feet are still on the spot!"

"They went up in the air when you fell!" I say. "You're out!"

"Swing Dare champion!" Rory yells, waving her arms from the swing and clapping as if she just won an Olympic event.

"Hey, guys!" We all turn to see my dad coming toward us. "What are you playing?"

Gabe gets up and brushes himself off. "Nothing anymore, because Rory cheats!"

"I do not! As long as I can land back in my spot, I'm safe."

"Good luck with that!" Gabe says.

"Well, if I can knock Maple out first, then it doesn't matter. I'll still win!"

"Those rules are stupid," Gabe says.

Rory moves her arms like she's swimming, trying to make the swing come at me.

"Uh, kids? This doesn't seem like a very nice game," my dad says. I wait for him to sing Mom's warning song, but he doesn't.

Rory ignores him and tries to grab me to pull me off my spot.

"Hey! That's cheating. You're supposed to knock me off with the tire! No hands!"

"I *am* the tire! I'm an extension of the tire!"

"You can't change the rules once we start," I say. "That's not fair!"

Rory ignores me and, as soon as she swings back toward me again, makes another grab. She manages to get hold of my shirt and pulls. I try to stay put, but as she swings away from me, she keeps hold of my shirt and stretches it away from my body. I scream for her to let go, but she holds tight.

"Gabe!" I say. "Help!"

Gabe runs over and tries to pull us apart, but it's no use and I fall forward.

"I win!" Rory says.

The neck of my T-shirt is all stretched out. It's one of my favorites. One of the few shirts that was not a hand-me-down but one I bought when Katy's dad took us to a Red Sox game last year. I used up all my birthday money to buy it.

"You jerk! You ruined my favorite shirt! Dad! Do something!"

Rory jumps out of the tire swing and pumps her fists in the air. "Vic-to-ry!"

"Dad!" Gabe says. "Aren't you going to say something?"

"Rory," he finally says. "That wasn't nice."

"Aw, it's just a T-shirt. Throw it in the wash and it'll get its shape back."

My dad looks at me, as if to see if that's enough to make things right.

It isn't! My eyes start to water. I know I'm going to cry any minute. I don't want Rory to see me, so I grab the swing and push it toward her with all my strength. She's still too busy doing her victory dance to notice, and the swing bonks her on the back and she falls over.

Gabe laughs so hard, he almost falls over, too.

"Maple!" my dad says, using that stern voice again. "That was mean!"

I'm in shock. "So what she did is OK, but I can't get her back?"

"Never return violence with violence," he says. "That doesn't solve anything."

"Seriously, Dad?" Gabe asks.

Rory gets up and brushes her own clothes off. There's a dirt mark on the front of her shirt. Good!

"Now we're even," she says. "Baby."

That does it. No one calls me a baby! I grab the swing again and get ready to launch it at her, but my dad grabs it.

"Stop!" he says. "I did not raise you kids to fight like this."

He looks genuinely angry now, and it makes me realize I've rarely seen my dad get mad. Usually, he just walks away when things get ugly. Now I've seen him angry twice in one day.

Gabe notices, too, and so does Rory. I can tell by the way their faces change, from angry to guilty.

"Sorry," Rory says. "I was only trying to have fun."

I step back and look at the ground. "Me too," I say. "Sorry."

"Why don't you kids try playing by the rules?" my dad says. "Line back up."

He takes a few steps backward, holding the tire.

"Are you playing with us?" Gabe asks, surprised.

He nods. "Tell me the rules."

We form a circle with him while Rory explains. This time, she leaves out all the extras she just added.

"Who thought of this game?" my dad asks.

"We all did," Rory said. "But mostly me, I guess."

"Hm," he says.

I don't want him to play this with us. It's not like Uno or Monopoly or some other family game. It's a game only siblings play. I don't want to throw something at my dad. Or have him throw something at me. It's different from throwing stuff at Rory and Gabe. I wish my mom would come out and interrupt us. Usually, she knows when we're about to do something that's going to make at least one of us cry. But then I remember *she* is the one who was crying earlier. Because of my dad. I wonder if they made up. I wonder why he came out here in the first place.

"I'm really supposed to try to knock you over with this?" my dad asks, still holding the tire. "That feels wrong."

"It doesn't hurt!" Rory says. "I mean, not really."

My dad holds the tire back and glances at each of us, one at a time, as if he's trying to decide who to take out first.

"This is weird," Gabe says. "Dad, let's play something else."

But instead, my dad swings the tire right at me.

Before I can jump out of the way, it hits me straight on and bonks my nose so hard that I fall back and land on my bum. I don't know why getting hit in the nose hurts so much, but it's truly the worst place to get hit. I think I see stars. I sit still, in too much pain to move.

"Maple!" my dad shouts. He dashes over to me. "Honey! I'm so sorry! I didn't mean to hurt you!"

"Dad wins!" Rory shouts. I know she's only kidding, but my dad looks shocked.

"Rory. Shame on you! How can you have so little empathy for your sister! She's hurt!"

"Sorry," Rory says quietly. "I was only joking. Are you OK?"

I close my eyes as my nose goes *whomp-whomp-whomp* in pain, but I nod. I don't want my dad to feel bad about hurting me. I know he didn't mean to.

He puts his hands on my shoulders. "Maple, look at me," he says.

I open my eyes, and he studies me closely. "Do you think it's broken?"

"What's broken?"

"Your nose, honey. Did you . . . hear a strange noise or anything when the tire hit you?"

I shake my head. "No, Dad. I'm OK."

But he looks concerned. And worried. And scared? His eyes start to water. I don't think I've ever really seen my dad cry before. "I'm so sorry, Mapes," he says. "I promise I didn't mean to hurt you!"

"I'm fine, Dad!" I stand up. I feel a little wobbly but try not to show it. "See?"

He shakes his head and stands up, too. "You kids," he says, disappointed. "I just don't understand your games."

It feels like none of us knows what to do now. What if we gave him one more thing to be upset about? One more thing to make him want to get away from us?

"Well," my dad says. "I guess I'll go back inside."

We watch him walk away.

"What a crappy day this turned out to be," Rory says.

"Yeah," Gabe agrees. "Thanks to you."

"Oh, come on. If Dad hadn't come out, everything would be fine. We were having fun!"

"Maybe you were," I say, looking down at my stretched-out shirt.

"Whatever," Rory says. She stomps off in a mood.

"Are you really OK?" Gabe asks me. "That looked like it hurt. A lot. You know Dad didn't mean to hurt you, right? And you know Rory. She gets carried away. I'm sure she didn't realize she was ruining your shirt."

Sometimes, when someone is nice to you or sees that you're sad, it's hard to keep the tears you've been holding in from spilling out all over.

"Maple!" Gabe says. "What is it?"

I gulp my sobs a bit and turn away from him.

"I'm fine!" I say. "Leave me alone!"

But he stays put, waiting.

When I'm all done, I wipe my face with my stretched-out, ruined T-shirt.

"Want me to go get you some tissues?" he asks.

I shake my head.

"Everything feels wrong and awful," I tell him. "Mom and Dad fighting. Rory being mean. I don't like it."

"I know," he says quietly.

"Do you think Mom and Dad will make up?"

"Of course they will. Don't they always?"

"I hate it when they fight."

"Me too."

We sit down at the foot of the tree and lean against the trunk. Every so often, the wind rustles the leaves a little, and they make a whisper sound, as if the tree is trying to comfort me again. I wish I could build a fort up in the branches right now and not have to wait until summer. The branches could really be like arms then, holding the platform up. Holding *me* up.

"I'm gonna go in now," Gabe says. "You coming?"

I shake my head. "Not yet."

He stands up and turns to me before going inside. "You sure you're OK?"

I nod, and he nods back. Then he leaves me in the shade and goes inside.

I reach around the tree for my sketchbook and slide out the Sharpie clipped inside the spiral spine. I press my back against the solid trunk and open my book. Some people probably think it's strange that my mom named me after a tree. I wish I was more like one. Strong and sturdy, with roots stretching so far into the ground, nothing could knock me over. My mom says when I do something sweet, she knows she named me right. Sweet like maple syrup. But today I don't feel that way at all. If anything, I feel like a fragile maple leaf, about to break away and fall from the sky.

Eighteen

When my mom calls us in to help with dinner, the mood in the kitchen feels a bit better.

"What are we having?" I ask, sniffing the air. "It smells spicy!"

"Chili!" my mom says. "You have a good nose."

My dad stops grating some cheese and leans toward me to inspect my face. "Feeling OK?" he asks. "Glad your nose still works."

I nod, and he gives me a squeeze and ruffles my hair. "I love you, kiddo."

"I love you, too," I say, feeling relieved that he seems like his old self.

"Want to be the can opener?" he asks, gesturing toward a bunch of bean cans.

"Sure." I open the first can and start on the next.

"Hey!" Gabe says, bouncing into the kitchen. "Table's all set. Need anything else?"

"Rinse the beans, please," my mom says.

"Ugh. They stink."

"But they taste delicious!" Rory says, coming up behind him. "Beans, beans, they're good for your heart, the more you eat, the more you—"

"Rory! Don't be gross," my mom says.

Rory clears her throat. "OK, fine. Beans, beans, the magical fruit, the more you eat, the more you—"

My mom swats her with a dish towel.

My dad makes a toot sound, and Rory cracks up.

"Don't encourage them!" my mom says jokingly.

He makes the noise again, right in my mom's ear. I can't tell if he's trying to be funny still or just plain mean, but my mom looks a little hurt by it.

Why did he have to do that? She was only kidding! Just when things were starting to seem fun again, he has to go and ruin it.

I finish opening the last can of beans and slam the can opener on the counter. Then I stomp out of the kitchen, grab my sketchbook off the table where I left it, and go to my room. I barely have time to open my book before there's a knock on my door.

"Honey?" my mom says.

I push my door open and she pokes her head in.

"You OK?"

"Why is Dad so mean to you all the time?" I ask, trying not to cry.

"Is that what you think?" She actually looks surprised. But I *know* she was hurt when he made that noise in her ear.

"Yes, he is. He's always telling you how you're no fun. But you are!"

"Oh, he doesn't mean it."

"It's still not nice to say! When Rory and Gabe say things like that to me, it really hurts my feelings, so I know what it's like."

She reaches into the closet to squeeze my knee.

"Do *not* say I'm too sensitive, Mom."

"I wasn't going to! I was going to say . . ."

But she stops. Her fingers gently press into my knee. It feels like we're holding hands but not.

"You were going to say it, weren't you?"

"No, honey. I was going to say that I don't think Dad tries to hurt my feelings."

"But he does hurt them. Doesn't he?"

Her fingers cling to me. I reach down and put my hand over hers.

"Sometimes," she says quietly. "But it doesn't count if he doesn't mean it."

"Yes, it does!" I say. "Mom! You've always taught us how powerful words are."

"Oh, Maple."

I crawl out from my closet and hug her. She smells like chili. "I don't like it when he treats you that way. He doesn't feel like Dad when he does that. He feels like a stranger."

"Maple, stop. Don't talk about Dad like that."

"But it's true!"

She holds me tight.

"I know you're fun, Mom. I know you care! You just don't want us to get hurt. Being cautious isn't the same as not being fun." I'm crying again, and my nose is running and it hurts. It hurts because my dad bonked it with a tire, even though he didn't mean to. I bury my face in her chili shirt.

"Maple, Maple, how I love thee," my mom sings. "Sweet as syrup, strong as a tree." It's a song she made up about me when I was a baby. It feels so good to be in her arms, held close. I want to be sweet and strong, like the tree I was named for. I want to help her feel better, the way my tree sometimes helps me.

"Dinner's getting cold!" Gabe calls from downstairs.

My mom lets go of me and pulls me up. "We all have bad days, and we all say things we don't mean sometimes. It's going to be fine."

"Promise?"

She nods and smiles but doesn't say yes. Rory would tell her that doesn't count. You have to say the words. But I just nod back and follow her downstairs.

Rory waves a bottle of hot sauce at me. "We're having a Firecracker Dare," she says. "Whoever puts the most drops in *and* finishes their chili wins." She drops a few in her bowl and takes it to the table.

"How many drops was that?" my dad asks.

"Five!"

My dad counts out seven and takes his bowl to the table.

Gabe picks up the bottle and reads the ingredients, then puts a drop on his finger to test how hot it is.

"It's not *that* bad," he says, and drops eight in his bowl.

My mom and I stare at the bottle.

"Someone's gonna end up cry-ing," my mom whisper-sings to me.

I smirk. "It won't be me," I say. "I don't like hot sauce. I'm out!"

"Me either," she says. "Let's go watch the show."

When we're all at the table, my mom says she's feeling extra grateful to be together and that we should take a moment to think about what else we're grateful for.

Dad says he's grateful for the musical fruit. Rory says spices. Gabe says doughnuts, even though Rory touched them all just to be a jerk. I say the Red Sox and give Rory a dirty look. Mom says artists and winks at me.

We all clink glasses and then dig in. Mom makes the best chili. I love the mixture of roasted peppers and tomatoes, and even the beans. Even though I wasn't hungry, as soon as I have a few bites, I can't stop because it's so delicious. Dad, Rory, and Gabe all started out wolfing their food down, but they've definitely slowed up. Rory drinks her entire glass of water and jumps up for more.

"Little hot?" Dad asks, grinning. It's nice to all be having fun again. With everyone in a good mood. Maybe I *was* overreacting earlier. Maybe I *am* too sensitive.

Gabe fans his face. "I'm sweating!" he says.

When Rory comes back, she looks to see how much is left in my dad's and Gabe's bowls. "I've totally got this," she says, sitting back down and taking another huge bite.

My dad whistles and smacks his lips. "That's hot," he says. "That's definitely hot. My lips are officially on fire."

"Can people die from overheating?" I ask. "Like, what if your throat is so hot, it closes up?"

My mom gets a worried look.

Rory takes a big gulp of her water. "Don't say that,

Maple! Yeesh. Way to spoil the mood." She turns to my dad. "That can't happen, right?"

"Of course not," my dad says. "Your sister's just a worrywart."

I scowl and look over at my mom, who shakes her head, as if to say, *Let it go.*

My dad takes a huge bite. "Almost there," he says.

Gabe shovels another spoonful in his mouth. "Is smoke coming out of my ears?" he asks with his mouth full. A little chili drips down his chin.

"Gross! Better lick that up or you'll be disqualified," Rory says, taking another bite. She wipes her forehead with her napkin. "Hot, hot, hot!"

My dad scrapes his bowl with his spoon and lifts it up to his mouth. "Last bite!" he says. "How much do you two have left?"

Rory lifts up her spoon and shoves another mouthful of chili in, then scrapes her bowl. But as she's chewing and trying to swallow, she suddenly stops midbite and coughs it all up, right back into her bowl!

"Rory!" my mom says. "Gross!"

"Good aim!" I say.

She coughs again and doesn't stop.

"Drink some water!" Gabe says, then shovels in a mouthful of his own. He chews fast and swallows.

My dad is still sitting there with his spoon at

his mouth, but he hasn't put it in yet. His nose is running.

"I win!" Gabe says, jumping up. His face is bright red and sweaty.

Rory coughs again and a big chunk of pepper comes out and plops into her bowl.

"Wow!" my dad says.

"I was choking!" Rory says. "No fair! The game should have paused! You didn't even realize I could be dying!"

"You seem fine now," my dad says.

Rory quickly scoops up the food she just spit out and shoves it back into her mouth. She washes it down with water and slams her empty glass on the table. "Second place!"

"Now that's dedication," I say.

"And also disgusting," Gabe points out.

"You kids are too much for me," my dad says, dropping his spoonful back into his bowl. "When did you become so competitive?"

"Rory, are you all right?" my mom asks, looking serious. "You should not eat after you choke!"

"Oh, calm down, Colleen," my dad says. "She's fine."

"My chest is on fire!" Rory says.

"That is not going to feel good coming out the other end," Gabe says.

My dad chuckles.

"What do you mean?" Rory asks.

Gabe stands up and sticks his butt out to show her.

"Ew!" I say.

"Mom!" Rory says. "Is it going to burn?"

I start laughing so hard, I get the hiccups.

"I suppose it might," my mom says. "I mean, they do say not to touch your eyes after you touch a hot pepper. Or . . . other places."

Rory looks panicked.

I laugh harder.

"Someone *is* gonna end up crying!" I say, and hiccup again.

"It's not funny!" Rory says.

My mom starts laughing, too. "People eat hot food every day," she says. "And it goes through them all the same way and they survive. Try drinking lots of water."

"Do we have any ice cream?" Gabe asks. "Maybe that would help."

"Good idea!" my dad says. He jumps up and runs into the kitchen, but comes back empty-handed. "No ice cream," he says. "I'll run out and get some!"

"Yes!" Gabe says. "Cookies and cream!"

"No! Mint chocolate chip! It will feel colder," Rory says.

"I'll get both!" He rushes over to the door and stops. "Any other requests?"

My mom and I shake our heads. "Just don't forget to bring your phone and make sure it's on," my mom says.

"Why?" my dad asks, his mood suddenly changing.

I hiccup again.

"Never mind," my mom says.

My dad rolls his eyes. "You always have to spoil a nice time, Colleen!" he calls over his shoulder. "Good job!" He slams the door behind him.

We all look at my mom. She closes her eyes and takes a deep breath, then lets it out. "Let's clean up while we wait," she says.

Rory rubs her belly. "I don't feel so good."

"Nice try," my mom says. "Now hustle your buns to the kitchen and bring your dirty dishes!"

After we clean up, we sit around the table, waiting for my dad to come back with the ice cream. A half hour goes by, and we decide to play cards to pass the time. But after three rounds of rummy, he's still not home.

"Text him!" Rory says.

"I did," my mom says. "No answer."

"Maybe he had to go to more than one store to find the right kind," I say.

"Maybe," my mom says. "Probably. I think the tank was low, he probably stopped to get gas, too."

"He left in kind of a huff," Gabe says.

"Let's not go there," my mom says.

We play another round, but my dad still doesn't show up. My mom starts pacing around the table and checking her phone every few minutes. This feels just like at the concert when he went off without telling anyone.

"I don't want to play anymore," Rory says. "I feel kind of sick. For real."

"Drink some more water and go lie down, then," my mom says. "I'll call up when Dad gets home."

Gabe and I play double solitaire a few times, then we give up, too. My mom comes and sits with us and plays a round by herself while we watch.

"I never win at this game," she says, gathering the cards and reshuffling them.

"You have to play at least seven times to win. Roughly," I tell her.

"How do you know that?"

"Because we tried it."

"You did?"

"Uh-huh," Gabe says. "We kept track in a notebook, and all three of us played with our own decks, and that's pretty much how many times you have to play, give or take."

"Think I have time to play that many times before your dad comes home?"

We shrug.

"Mom," Gabe says. "Where do you think Dad is?"

"Oh, I don't know. You know Dad. Sometimes he just decides to go for a drive to blow off steam."

"But he was supposed to go get ice cream. He could at least text to let you know where he is," Gabe says. "Why does he get so angry lately?"

My mom sighs. "I don't know, honey. I shouldn't have made that comment about the phone."

"It's not *your* fault."

"Who wants to watch a movie?" she asks, changing the subject.

"Me!" I say.

The three of us cuddle on the couch, and Mom finds an old favorite, *The Princess Bride*.

I get out my sketchbook to draw while we watch.

"How can you draw and watch at the same time?" Gabe asks. "You're missing half the movie."

"It helps me listen," I say.

"Let her be, Gabe," my mom says. "She's not hurting you."

I shift on the couch so Gabe can't see my pages, and we keep watching. I don't know why Gabe cares, anyway. We've seen this movie a hundred times!

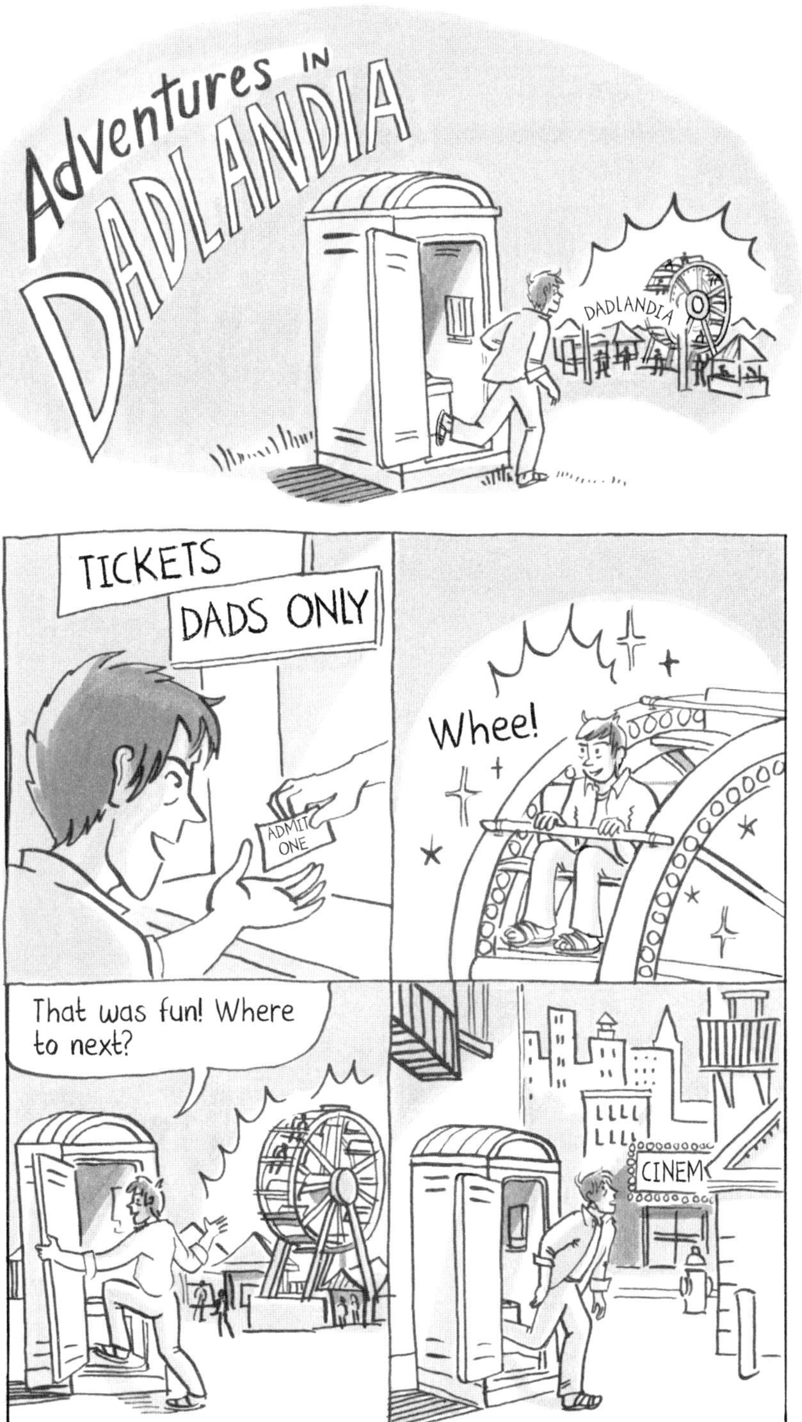

Nineteen

My dad returns halfway through the movie. As soon as the headlights from the car flash through the window, my mom tells us to go up to bed.

"What about the ice cream?" Gabe asks.

"Up!" my mom says.

I follow Gabe up, but we wait in the hallway to listen. My parents whisper-yell at each other, but they shouldn't bother trying to be quiet because we can hear everything. We're there for just a few minutes before Rory joins us.

"I just don't understand you anymore," my mom says. "This isn't like you!"

"You keep pushing my buttons!" my dad says. "It's like you can't help yourself. I just needed to go somewhere and think."

"Think about what? How annoyed you are with me? Just because I asked you to bring your phone with you? You keep doing this and it's not fair. It's not fair to me or the kids."

"I only went for a drive, Colleen. Could you just relax, already? This is exactly what I mean."

"Don't tell me to relax! I would relax if I knew where you were, Dan! You told the kids you'd bring them ice cream."

"I forgot! They aren't babies. Besides, I got them doughnuts this morning. How many treats do they need?"

"They don't *need* them. But you promised!"

"I didn't promise. I just said I would get some."

"And you didn't! You didn't do what you said you would. Again."

It's quiet for a minute. Rory's and Gabe's breathing next to me sounds extra loud as we wait.

"I hate this," my mom finally says.

"Why don't you say what you really hate?" my dad says.

"And what would that be?"

"Me."

"Oh, that's rich, coming from the person who's always putting me down."

"I don't put you down!"

"Really? 'You're no fun, Colleen. Lighten up, Colleen.' Just admit it, Dan. You're the one who hates me. Lately it seems like you can't stand to be near me."

It's quiet again. And then there's what sounds like my mom crying. I feel the ache of a sob in my own chest.

Beside me, I can feel Rory's breath in my hair, we're so close. Gabe puts his hand on my shoulder, as if to keep me from running down the stairs and begging my parents to make up.

"I'm sorry," my dad says. "But I'm no good at this. I told you I wouldn't be."

"Good at what?" my mom asks.

"*This*. Being a family man. Having all these responsibilities. Working at a job I hate just so we can have family health insurance."

"But you said you wanted the job. You said it felt good working for a company that cared for the environment."

"Too bad they don't care about the stress they put their sales force under! And then to come home only to have you make me feel even worse—"

"How do I make you feel worse? I've never said anything about your job!"

"You don't have to! It's the way you look at me! The way you're always worried about money. You think I can't see how disappointed you are that I don't do enough?

Provide enough? Do you ever wonder what that feels like?" My dad swears, and I can hear keys jingle, as if he's getting ready to go for another drive.

"Seriously?" my mom says. "You're taking off again? Must be nice to just hop in the car every time things get tough instead of talking things through. Meanwhile, I have to stay here and—" She stops, as if taking a deep breath. "No. No. I'm sorry. Dan, I'm sorry I've made you feel bad. Please stay so we can talk about this. The Kleebers got couples therapy a few years ago. Beth and Sam both said it did wonders for th—"

"We don't need therapy, Colleen. I know what the problem is."

"Well, tell me, then! Tell me so we can fix this!"

"This isn't fixable."

Some footsteps creak toward the bottom of the stairs, and the three of us race to Gabe's room, which is the closest, to hide.

My dad's feet pound up the stairs. We hear him go into the bathroom and shut the door. Then we hear quieter steps follow and go into my parents' bedroom.

The three of us sit in the dark on Gabe's bed, waiting. Too afraid to speak.

We wait and listen. It's so quiet, I can hear Rory's stomach growl. She burps, and the whole room suddenly smells like nasty chili.

"You are so gross!" Gabe hisses.

"Sorry!" she says. "I can't help it!"

Gabe and I quietly slide as far away from Rory on the bed as possible.

"At least it's not coming out the other end," Rory whispers. "I bet that would be a lot worse."

"Shh!" Gabe says.

We hear the bathroom door open and footsteps again, but they don't go to the bedroom—they go downstairs. After a few minutes, we hear my mom leave the bedroom and go downstairs, too. We all creep out to the hallway and try to hear them again, but the house is quiet.

"What do we do?" I ask.

"I have to go to the bathroom," Rory says, and hurries down the hall.

"Let's go back to my room," Gabe says.

His window is open, and the moon shining through makes his room glow pale. We sit on the floor and lean against his bed. A soft breeze that smells like new leaves comes through the window screen. I imagine my tree leaning toward the window to listen and check on us.

"I'm scared," I say.

"Me too," Gabe says.

"Why is Dad so upset? Why does he think Mom is so disappointed?"

"I don't know," Gabe says.

"What if . . . what if he doesn't love Mom anymore? Or . . . us?"

"Don't say that."

"Why does he keep needing to get away from us?"

"I don't know," he says again.

"What if we told him we'd be better? We could promise to stop playing games that upset him. And promise to be nicer to each other."

"We could try."

I nod. "OK. Let's tell him in the morning. That we're sorry. And we'll try harder."

"Good idea."

The toilet flushes, and a few seconds later Rory staggers into the room.

"Do not go into the bathroom unless it's a life-or-death situation," she says.

"Did it burn?" I ask.

"I don't want to talk about it."

Another breeze comes through the window. I take a deep breath of it before Rory can stink the place up again with her burps.

"Why is Dad being such a jerk?" Rory asks.

"Don't say that!" I say.

"Well, it's true! He loses his temper at the drop of a

hat. Mom can't seem to say anything without him getting all mad. Do you think that's fair?"

"No," I say.

"Well, there you go."

"He's selfish," Gabe says. "That's his problem."

"That's not nice!" I say.

"Neither is storming off whenever he gets annoyed, leaving us all to worry," Gabe says.

"What did Mom mean about getting therapy like the Kleebers?" I ask.

"It's like when people are having marriage problems, and they try to get help from a marriage counselor," Rory says.

"It sounded like it helped the Kleebers. Maybe it could help Mom and Dad," I say hopefully.

"Maybe," Gabe says. "But Dad didn't exactly sound like he was willing to try it."

We hear footsteps on the stairs again, but only one person walks down the hall. Mom's slippers. We don't move, holding our breath until she passes so she doesn't know we're up. When she shuts their bedroom door, we all breathe out at the same time.

"Where do you think Dad is now?" I ask.

A door slams and we all rush to Gabe's window to look out at the backyard, lit only by the moon. We watch our dad walk over to the tire swing. He grabs hold and steps back, lifting it as high as his head. Then swings it, hard, at the tree.

"No!" I gasp.

"Shh!" Rory hushes me.

The tree branches rustle.

Dad lifts the tire again. Over and over, he slams the tire against the tree.

When we were little and got into fights, my dad always told us if we were tempted to hit each other, go hit something you can't hurt. Even though he's not hitting anyone, it hurts to watch. It hurts to see him so angry. It hurts to watch him hit my tree.

Tears stream down my face, but I don't make a sound. Rory and Gabe watch quietly. I don't know when, but at some point, Rory takes my hand. She squeezes it now, and I can see the side of her face is soaked in tears, too.

Gabe doesn't move from the window. None of us do. We just watch our dad, tiring himself out. Finally, he lets go of the tire and drops to his knees. He looks up at the branches, as if he's praying to them or asking for forgiveness. He stays that way for a long, long time. Then he gets up and walks around the other side of the house where we can't see him.

"What do we do?" Rory asks. "Should we go after him?"

"No," Gabe says. "He wants to be alone. Obviously."

We move away from the window and slide back over to our spots on the floor.

After a while, we hear my parents' bedroom door open again. My mom shuffles down the hall and stops in Gabe's doorway. She looks surprised to see us. And tired. So tired.

"Kids," she says. "What's going on?"

"Is Dad leaving us?" Rory asks.

My mom grips each side of the door frame, as if to hold herself up. She takes a deep breath. Is she deciding whether she should lie, too?

"Dad loves you," she says. "You know that, right? We'll work this out."

"Where is he now?" Gabe asks. "Is he waiting downstairs to have a family discussion?" The tone of his voice is more salty than sassy. It's angry. And scared.

My mom looks as surprised to hear it as I am.

"What are you trying to say?" she asks.

"We just watched him beat up the tree!" Gabe says. "And now he's gone off again. Good dads don't do that!"

"Gabe!" my mom says.

"He doesn't love us anymore, does he, Mom?" I ask.

"Oh, Maple. Of course he does! What has gotten into you kids? Why are you talking this way?"

"We heard your conversation," Rory says. "Or most of it, anyway. Dad said things aren't fixable. He wants to get away from us."

"That's . . . that's not true! Your father loves you very much. When he says he needs space, it doesn't mean he doesn't love you or want to be with you anymore."

"Then what does it mean?" Gabe asks.

My mom walks into the room and sits on Gabe's bed. In the darkened room, she looks like a big shadow. "He's overwhelmed and needs some space, that's all. And it's me he's frustrated with, not you."

"Seems to me that if you love people, you stick with them and work things out together."

"Gabe." There's a warning sound in my mom's voice. "I'm doing the best I can to be open and honest with you. You all have friends whose parents have gone through rough patches. This is just . . . one of those times. I don't know what else to tell you, other than it doesn't mean Dad loves the three of you any less."

We all sit quietly for a minute. As we do, a horrible smell fills the room.

"What . . . what is that smell?" my mom asks.

I plug my nose.

"Sorry," Rory says.

Gabe waves his hands in the air and runs over to the window.

"Uh-oh!" Rory gets up and runs down the hall.

"Feel the burn!" Gabe calls after her.

"You kids," my mom says. "You need to go to bed."

Twenty

In the morning, Rory still has "chili effects," as she calls them, so my mom says she can stay home from school. Then my mom decides to let us all stay home since Gabe and I point out that we ate the same thing and it's only a matter of time before we start having chili effects, too. After breakfast, we help my mom pick up, and then she orders us all to clean our rooms and strip our beds. When my mom is worried, she cleans. Everything. Every time we hear a noise outside, one of us runs to the window to see if Dad has come back, but it's never him.

Finally, in the late afternoon, my mom gathers us

together. She's holding her phone and tells us she's heard from Dad. He's going to stay at a friend's place for the night.

"What friend?" I ask.

"Peter. You know, Dad's old friend. He has that cabin we visited last year, remember? On the lake? He's letting Dad stay there."

"All alone?" Gabe asks.

My mom nods.

"Just for the night?" Rory asks.

"I'm not sure," my mom says.

She presses her lips together like she's trying not to cry.

Gabe swears and throws the rag he was dusting with on the floor.

"Gabe! Pick that up!" My mom doesn't yell very often, so when she does, you know she's really angry.

Gabe quickly picks up the rag and mutters, "Sorry."

"I know this is upsetting," my mom says more gently. She sits down on the couch with a thud. "Your dad says he thinks we need a little break. Him and me, I mean. I'm sorry."

Rory and I go and sit on either side of her. I lean my head against her shoulder.

"Can I read his text?" Rory asks.

My mom hesitates, then hands her the phone.

"It says he loves us," Rory says. She hands the phone back to my mom, looking relieved.

Gabe rolls his eyes. My mom notices but doesn't tell him to knock it off, like she usually would.

"Of course he loves you," my mom says.

"Then why is he staying at Peter's cabin?" I ask. "Why won't he come home?"

"Because he loves himself more," Gabe says, crossing his arms at his chest and leaning against the wall across from us.

"Gabe, honestly," my mom says. "Is that fair?"

"Fair?" Gabe asks, stepping forward. "Why should I be fair when Dad's being such a jerk?"

"Gabe!" My mom sits forward, too. "Please don't say that. Dad's upset with me, not you kids."

My mom sinks back against the couch again. I press my head harder against her shoulder. She reaches around and hugs me close. Her body starts to shake a little and she sniffs, like she's trying not to cry.

"It's OK to let it out," I tell her. "We can handle it."

She laughs and cries at the same time. "Oh, Maple," she says.

"If Dad doesn't come back tonight, can we stay home from school again tomorrow?" Rory asks.

My mom wipes her face with her free hand. "No, honey. Sorry."

"But what if Dad comes back and his feelings are hurt because we aren't here?" I ask.

"He's not coming back," Gabe says. "So it doesn't matter."

"Gabe! What has gotten into you? Dad is coming back!" My mom seems angry all over again.

"When?" Gabe says, sounding equally angry. "Did he say?"

My mom hesitates.

"You read the text, Rory," Gabe says in a know-it-all voice. "When is Dad coming home?"

"He didn't say," Rory says quietly.

"But he is!" I yell. "Right, Mom?"

"Of course he is," she says. "This is just for a few days at most."

Gabe shakes his head like he doesn't believe her, then stomps off.

"I should go talk to him," my mom says.

"No, I will," Rory says.

My mom looks surprised.

"Don't worry, I'll be nice." Rory gets up and follows in Gabe's direction. I hear the screen door slam and imagine they're both going out back to see the Ganders and talk.

"Guess it's just you and me," my mom says. "You want to practice your math with me?"

I shake my head. "I don't need to practice. I know the answers."

"I know you do, honey. I just thought—"

"I don't want to, Mom."

"OK. Do you want to come help me figure out what to make for dinner?"

I shake my head again. "I'm going to draw for a while."

She gives me a squeeze and gets up. "All right, honey. That sounds like a good idea."

I find my sketchbook and go outside to my tree. I know it's silly, but I set my sketchbook down and give the tree a hug.

"I'm sorry he hurt you," I whisper to the tree. "He didn't mean it."

I sit down and lean against the trunk, pressing my back against it. I think about my dad and wonder what he's doing right now at Peter's cabin on the lake. We've been there a few times, and I try to remember what it looked like. There was a hammock and lots of trees. And a kayak for taking out on the water. We had fun going there, but I can't imagine being there all alone, with no one to talk to or play with.

"Please let him be OK," I say to the tree. "Please tell him to come home."

The breeze shakes the tree's branches a little, and I imagine it's taking in my wish and then maybe sending the message out to my dad somehow.

Our science teacher told us once that trees know how to communicate with one another. Their roots have a whole network under the ground, and they help each other know how big to grow—how wide and how tall. I imagine my wish entering the tree's leaves as if they are thousands of ears, then sending the message along the branches, down the trunk, and underground, out through the roots, for miles and miles and miles, from one tree to the next, until they reach whatever tree I imagine my dad sitting under right now. Maybe he's swinging in the hammock, missing us. I imagine my wish making its way up through the roots of the tree he's under. It goes through those roots, up the trunk, and out the branches to the leaves, who whisper in the air so my dad can hear them.

Go home, Dan.
Go home.
Maple needs you. Your family needs you.

Twenty-One

"I can't believe you're making us go to school when Dad's missing," Rory says from the front seat on the way to school the next morning.

"He's not missing," my mom says, annoyed.

"Well, he's not here!" Gabe says.

"Gabe," my mom says. "Please don't."

"Don't what?"

"Make things worse," I say. "Can't you tell Mom is sad?"

Gabe smacks his head against the headrest behind him. "This sucks," he says.

"Gabriel!" my mom says. "You know I don't like that word."

He rolls down his window and tilts his head out, just a little. But not like a happy dog, the way Rory taught us. "Well, it does," he says into the breeze.

"It's true," Rory says. "It sucks."

I reach forward and pat my mom's shoulder. She takes one hand from the steering wheel to give mine a squeeze.

"I know," she says.

Katy and Astrid are already at school in the drop-off zone, waiting.

I'm shocked to see the ABC's standing with them.

"Maple!" Astrid yells, and runs toward me. "Where were you yesterday?"

Katy follows behind, and they take my hands, like usual.

"Aren't you three a little old to hold hands?" one of the ABC's says. Dora is standing with them, holding one of their hands. She fidgets and pulls away, then runs over to take Astrid's free hand instead.

"It's not for safety. It's for friendship," Astrid says matter-of-factly. "And it's a private joke between us."

"Yeah," Katy says, swinging our arms high.

"Let's run!" I say, pulling on their hands.

We start to race up the sidewalk, but the crossing guard yells at us and makes us stop.

"You guys are weird," one of the ABC's says.

I wish I could tell them apart. I remember now that Bryce has a little scar on his forehead. And one wears a necklace with a charm on it that the other two don't. Charlie! That's it. So the other one is Adam. Today he's wearing a purple T-shirt. I try to study him more closely to come up with something that sets him apart so I can remember him, but then he catches me staring at him and I blush.

I squeeze Astrid's and Katy's hands tighter, and we speed-walk with Dora the rest of the way to the door. It's already hot this morning, and by the time we get to the entryway, our hands are sweaty. We let go and wipe them on our shorts.

"Have a great day!" Dora says to us. She waves to her brothers and skips inside.

"Did you hear we're having another division quiz today?" Charlie asks as the rest of us go inside. "I heard Ms. Kent might start giving us one every day now." Charlie is smart and always gets special recognition for his good grades. I bet he would get Student of the Month every month if it was allowed.

"Ugh," I say. "Just my luck."

"You can do it," he says. He touches the charm on his necklace.

"What is that?" I ask.

"Oh," he says. "It's something my uncle made." He holds it up so I can look closely.

"Is that a maze?" I ask.

"A labyrinth. You can trace the path with your fingers. It helps me calm down when I get nervous. My uncle says it's good for grounding you."

"That's really nice."

"Thanks."

I wonder why he has one and not Adam and Bryce, but I don't have time to ask because the bell rings and we all have to hurry to class.

I go straight to my seat and pull out my pencils. I sharpen them and then start to say division problems in my head.

Ms. Kent walks around and places our quiz papers facedown on our desks as usual, then goes to the front of the room with her timer. I think of Captain Ladybug taking it apart again and smile to myself, then feel a little guilty.

I turn back to give Parker a reassuring smile. He looks about as miserable as I feel.

"Take your time and think carefully before you write down each answer," Ms. Kent tells us. "Then you won't need to spend any time erasing."

I bet she is saying that for me and no one else.

"Ready? Begin."

The sound of papers flipping over fills the room, then the dreaded *clickety-clickety-click* of the timer. I look down at the first question. Before I write anything, I say the answer in my head, as if Gabe shouted out the question to me in the car.

Nine.

OK. I press my pencil to the paper. Circle, line down. I did it!

Next one: *Three.*

Loop one, loop two.

I keep going. Soon, I get all the way to the last problem. Just as I finish making a five, the kitchen timer goes off.

I look up. Astrid, Katy, and the ABC's are all staring at me. I scan my answers. I answered every single question and didn't erase any!

Ms. Kent gathers all the papers as she weaves up and down the aisles between desks.

"Nice job, Maple!" she says when she holds my paper up. She scans my answers right there in the middle of the aisle. My heart thumps nervously in my chest. When she finishes, she smiles and gives me a little nod to let me know I passed.

Charlie shows me a thumbs-up, and Astrid whispers, "Way to go!"

When Ms. Kent collects Parker's quiz, she does not give him a nod. I feel bad. I look over at him, and he frowns and shrugs at me. I roll my eyes to show him I think the whole thing is silly.

After school, Astrid and I get on the bus, and I follow her down the aisle.

"Astwid!" Dora calls. "Sit with me!"

We squeeze in with her, and she shows us a collage she made at school. It's a house she assembled with squares of crepe paper she glued to a piece of construction paper.

"See?" she says. "This is my house." She points to different windows. "That's the boys' room," she says, touching a window. Her finger still has dried glue on it. "And that's Gwammy's room. And that's mine."

"Who's Gwammy?" Astrid asks.

"Grammy," Bryce says from the seat behind us. "Our grandmother."

"Oh! Does your grandmother live with you?" Astrid asks.

"Mm-hmm. She's nice."

"She moved in with us after our gramps died so she wouldn't be alone," Charlie explains.

"You have a big family," Astrid says. "I can't imagine living in a house with that many people."

"It can be pretty loud," Charlie says. "But it's nice."

I wish when my house got loud, it was nice and not because my parents were arguing.

"I need my alone time," Astrid says.

"You won't find it at our house," Adam says. "Alone time just does not exist there."

"Why is it so important to be alone?" I ask Astrid. "It sounds lonely."

"Not at all. It gives me space to think."

She sounds just like my dad.

"What do you think about?" Charlie asks.

"I don't know. Things."

"What kinds of things?"

"Just . . . things."

I wonder what my dad is thinking about right now. I wonder if he's happier, being away from us.

"Bor-ing," Bryce sings. "Why would anyone want to be alone?"

"It is not boring!" Astrid says. "It's important. Everyone needs it."

"Not me!"

"Maybe you should try it before judging me," Astrid says.

"I wasn't judging you!" Bryce looks annoyed. "It just seems kind of silly."

"You just did it again! Silly? My feelings are not silly. And you think singing 'boring' at me isn't judging?"

He frowns. "I didn't mean it. Sorry."

"Can I come visit Jud again soon?" Dora asks, changing the subject.

Astrid eyes the ABC's, like she's trying to decide if she fully trusts them yet. "Sure."

"Yay! Do you have a pet, Maple?" Dora asks me. "I want a dog!"

Dora is so cute. Sometimes I wish I had a little sibling and didn't have to be the youngest.

"No," I say. "But I wish we did. Gabe is allergic, so we can't have pets."

"Well," Astrid says, "you could get the kind that have hair instead of fur."

"We can't afford a purebred," I say.

"Then, a rescue."

I shrug.

I don't think Astrid's family has to think about how much things cost as much as my family does. It's kind of annoying. Rory would say I'm just jealous. But that's not it. Not exactly, anyway.

I open my sketchbook and quickly draw a silly comic of Dora riding Jud. I carefully tear out the page and fold it, and when I get to my stop, I hand it to her. She looks shocked and pleased when I do, like I just gave her a surprise present. It feels good, knowing I made her smile. It makes *me* smile. And I realize it feels like a long time since I did that.

Twenty-Two

When we get to my stop, I race up the driveway, but of course Gabe and Rory get there first, as usual.

"No snacks again!" Gabe hollers from the kitchen. "Why don't we ever have any good snacks?"

Rory and I look in all the cupboards but don't find much.

"I wish Dad had gotten the ice cream like he promised," Rory says.

"He didn't promise," Gabe points out. "He just got distracted by being mad for no good reason."

"Don't talk about Dad like that," I say. "It's not nice."

"Let's walk to the store," Rory suggests, changing the subject away from Dad. "It's not that far. I still have birthday money. I'm craving chips!"

"I have too much homework," Gabe says. "You and Maple go."

"I don't want to go," I say. "I'm not that hungry."

"Fine. I'll go myself," Rory says. "But I'm not sharing if I have to do all the work!" She opens the door and then leans back in. "You'll regret this!" she says, and slams it behind her.

I walk over to the counter and pick up the notepad to check if my dad left a note about getting stuff out for dinner, then I remember he's not here. "Oh yeah," I say, setting it back down.

Gabe grabs the pad and tosses it across the room. It hits a cupboard and falls on the floor, pages all splayed. When he turns toward me, his cheeks are already wet with tears. Gabe hardly ever cries in front of me, and it feels awful to see.

"I hate him!" he yells. "He's so selfish! All he cares about is himself!"

"That's not true!" I say. "He cares about us!" I pick up the pad and try to fix the pages.

"Oh, really? He sure has a funny way of showing it!"

"Dad can't help the way he feels," I say. This sounds like something Gabe would usually tell me, not the other way around. The words don't feel right in my mouth. Like a lie. I want to believe them, but they don't seem quite right.

"Don't make excuses for him like Mom does!" Gabe yells. "He doesn't deserve it!"

"But—"

"Does *Mom* ever walk out on us? Does she take off without telling us where she's going? Does she go off to stay at a friend's and not even tell us when she's coming home?"

I try to imagine my mom doing any of the things my dad has done lately and can't.

"The answer is no!" Gabe cries before I can answer. "Because she cares about us! She feels responsible for us! We matter to her! Even if she was upset with Dad for something, she wouldn't take off and leave us!"

"Gabe," I say, tears blurring my own eyes. "Please don't say those things." Gabe is supposed to be the rational one. He always makes me feel better when I'm nervous or afraid. He always knows how to calm me down.

"Well, they're true!" he yells. "And I'm sick of pretending that everything is OK! It's not!"

"Stop it!" I plead. "You're scaring me!"

"Well, I'm scared, too!" He pounds his fist on the counter. "And I'm mad!"

I wish our mom was home to make things better and help Gabe calm down. She'd know the right thing to say.

Maybe even Rory could.

But me? What do I know?

"Dad cares about us," I say. "I know he does."

"Sometimes I wish I could be as naive as you are, Maple. I really do. Maybe then I wouldn't be so disappointed all the time." He leaves me in the kitchen, stomping so loudly, I can hear him go all the way through the living room and up the stairs.

I wipe my eyes and put the pad of paper where it belongs. Then I get my sketchbook out of my backpack and take it outside to my tree.

• • •

"Kids!" my mom calls out.

I quickly shut my sketchbook and go to greet her. She has a bag of takeout for dinner from our favorite Mexican restaurant, and she even got nachos.

"Where is everyone?" my mom asks as she puts all her things down on the counter.

"Gabe's upstairs and Rory's not back yet," I tell her.

"Where did she go?"

"She decided to walk to the store to get some snacks because we're all out."

My mom makes a worried face and looks at her phone. "When did she leave?"

I shrug. "When we got home from school."

"That was two hours ago!"

I don't admit that I lost track of time while I was drawing.

"What store did she go to?"

"She didn't say, but probably Jesse's, where we always go. They have the best snacks."

"It shouldn't have taken her this long to go there and back."

"Maybe she ran into a friend?"

"I don't like it when you kids go somewhere without telling me."

"Sorry."

"Well, it's not *your* fault." She sends Rory a text. But as soon as she does, we hear a *ding* and look over to see Rory's phone on the counter, plugged into the outlet.

"She didn't take her phone?" my mom says, panic in her voice.

"I guess she needed to charge it," I say. "It'll be OK."

She looks doubtful. "Maybe we should go try to find her."

"No, Mom. I'm sure she'll be back any minute." But now I'm worried, too.

When my mom worries, she fidgets. And right now, she cannot stop. She gets out plates for dinner, then utensils and serving spoons. Then rearranges them. Then moves the takeout bag from one end of the counter to the other. All this time, she paces back and forth nervously.

"Do you want me to ride my bike and go find her?" I ask.

"No!" she says. "I don't want to have to worry about you, too!"

"You don't have to worry! I'm always careful!"

She pauses and smiles at me. "I know, honey. I'm sorry. Um, I'm just going to take a quick drive down there to pick her up."

"Can I come?"

"Sure."

She calls up to Gabe to tell him we'll be right back,

and then we get in the car. It's not often I get to be alone in the car with my mom. Or really be alone with her ever. But instead of feeling nice, it feels kind of miserable.

We drive to Jesse's and don't see a sign of Rory on the way, so we park and go in to ask if she's been there. When we do, we find Rory standing at the counter talking to Jesse, eating from a huge bag of cheese puffs. Her fingers are bright orange, and she has orange cheese bits all over the front of her T-shirt. My mom stops in her tracks, and I brace myself for her to start screaming at Rory right in the middle of the store.

"Hi!" Jesse says, waving a cheese puff at us.

He's not the Jesse the store's named for. He's young Jesse, the original Jesse's grandson. He's a year older than Rory. Rory has a crush on him, but she doesn't know I know. I heard her talking to her best friend, Rosa, about him and how she loves his *dimples*.

Instead of yelling at Rory, my mom runs over to her and hugs her. The bag crinkles, and Rory coughs on a cheese puff. "Mom!" she says, and coughs again. "Stop!"

My mom lets go and steps back. "I was so worried about you! Why didn't you text to tell me where you were going?"

"My phone needed to be charged. I didn't think it was a big deal," Rory says. "It's just the store!"

She looks embarrassed about my mom making such a fuss, but I think it's way less embarrassing than getting yelled at.

"Did you pay for those?" my mom asks.

"Of course!"

"OK, then let's get going. I brought takeout home, and it's going to get cold."

Rory waves to Jesse, trying to act cool.

I make Rory sit in the back with me when we drive home. At the stop sign before we get to our house, I notice my mom's hands shaking as she tries to clutch the steering wheel.

"Mom?" I ask. "Are you OK?"

"I'm fine," she says. "I was just more worried than I realized."

"You worry too much," Rory says. She sounds just like my dad when he says "You're no fun." Like my mom worried for nothing.

My mom swings her head around and glares at her.

"Do not say that!" she says. "Do not ever say that!"

I turn to look at Rory, too.

"Why?" she asks. She looks genuinely confused.

"I worry because I love you!" my mom says. "And I was afraid something had happened!"

Rory cringes. "Sorry," she says.

My mom closes her eyes and takes a deep breath

before driving through the intersection. Good thing there aren't any other cars on the road.

We pull into the driveway, but my mom doesn't turn off the car. "One thing before we get out," she says.

We wait.

"Never assume something isn't a big deal, all right? Because it is. It is a big deal. We have an agreement, and you didn't follow through—and it meant I was worried sick until we found you."

"I'm sorry," Rory says. "Really."

My mom turns off the car and opens her door. "Just don't do that again," she says, and gets out.

"I won't," Rory says, following her. "I promise."

My mom nods and then hugs Rory again. I rush over and hug them both so hard, Rory squirms and pulls away.

"I had no idea you loved me so much!" she says. "Yeesh. Maybe I should disappear more often."

"Don't you dare!" my mom says, finally smiling. "Now get inside so we can have dinner."

Even though we're all in a better mood, nothing feels right when we sit down for dinner. Without my dad, the table feels off-balance. There's a missing piece at one end. I keep waiting for him to walk in and say, "Surprise! I'm back!" and act like nothing happened. But he doesn't. And I'm starting to wonder when he ever will.

Twenty-Three

The next day on our drive to school, we're all quiet. I don't think we've ever been this quiet in the car, all at once, in my life. We each stare out the windows and watch the familiar neighborhoods on our route to school. It seems strange, my mom driving us again instead of my dad. It seems wrong.

My mom grips the steering wheel and curses each time a traffic light turns yellow before we make it through. That's the only sound.

When we get to the drop-off area at my school, my mom pulls over and turns in her seat.

"Have a good day today, honey," she says to me.

Rory reaches over and punches my arm in a playful way. "Let's make a good snack together after school, OK?"

Gabe stares out his window, not looking at us.

"Whatever," I say. I get out and shut the door, then watch them pull away.

Astrid and Katy skip up to me the minute I reach the walkway. I haven't told them yet about my dad. I don't know why. I know they would be nice and try to make me feel better. Maybe that's why?

"Maple!" Katy says. "Happy second-to-last week of— Wait. What's wrong?"

She and Astrid stare at me.

"Nothing," I say. But I can't hide it. As soon as they both take my hands to do our usual run up the walk, the feeling of sadness and worry I held inside all the way to school bubbles up and leaks out of my eyes.

"Maple!" Astrid says. "What is it?"

I don't like to cry in front of anyone and especially not my friends, but suddenly I'm not just crying—I'm sobbing like a little baby, and it only gets worse the more embarrassed I am.

Katy pulls me close, and I hide my face in her neck.

"I'm sorry!" I say between sobs.

"It's OK. Let it out." She rubs my back like my mom would. I feel Astrid's arms around me, too. They hold me like that until the sobs run out and I can wipe my face with the back of my hand.

"Wow," Astrid says. "That was a lot. What's going on?"

"I don't really want to talk about it," I say.

Katy squeezes my shoulder. "That's what everyone says. But it always feels better to share. We're your best friends!"

Why does it feel like as long as you don't talk about something, there's this hope that maybe it's not real? Like maybe we're just imagining that Dad left us. Maybe he ran out of gas and can't get home. Maybe he was kidnapped. Maybe he really is trapped in Dadlandia. I could almost believe it, if my mom hadn't shared the text he sent.

"You don't really have to tell us if you don't want to," Astrid says. "But I agree with Katy that you'll probably feel better if you do."

I wipe my face again to make sure all the tears are gone. The morning school bell rings, and we realize we're going to be late if we don't sprint to the door.

"Later!" I say. And we all take off, not holding hands.

"No running, girls!" the crossing guard yells as we speed past.

"But we're late!" Katy calls over her shoulder.

We get to the door and hurry inside and speed-walk to our lockers. When I open mine, an envelope falls out. It's similar to the one Oliver gave me when he invited me to his party. I quickly shove it in my backpack and hurry to class.

Ms. Kent is already placing quizzes facedown on our desks when we get to our room, so I guess Charlie was right. A quiz every day until we all reach the goal. I rush to my chair and pull out my pencils to make sure they're sharp. When I look over at Parker, he gives me a thumbs-up, as if this time, for some reason, he's going to pass. Maybe he thinks if I could do it yesterday, he can, too. As soon as the timer starts, I remember what worked last time and try to go slow and steady, but all I can think about is Gabe being so quiet and upset. And my dad not being home. And what's going to happen if he decides to stay in Dadlandia forever. Before I know it, the buzzer goes off, and I've barely answered any questions.

Ms. Kent walks up and down the aisles collecting papers. "Great job, Parker!" she says when she picks up his paper. "I knew you could do it!"

I'm happy for Parker, but this means I'm probably the only one who messed up. A hot feeling in my chest starts to stir. The closer Ms. Kent gets to my desk the worse it feels, like something is boiling in there. I could have passed! I know the answers! I just couldn't concentrate. She doesn't say anything when she picks up my paper, but

I can feel Ms. Kent's disappointment. I want to scream. In fact, I can feel the boiling thing in my chest starting to move up into my throat like it is about to explode out of me. I quickly jump up and hurry down the aisle toward the door.

"Maple Owens, where do you think you're going without permission!"

I just keep going because I know if I open my mouth, words of regret, as Rory calls them, will escape and only make things worse. I run down the hall to the bathroom and find an open stall. Then I let it out. "Arrrrrrrrrrgh!"

It feels good but also scary. Any minute, I expect a teacher to come racing in to either yell at me or ask me what's wrong. But no one comes, and I just stand there, feeling the empty place in my chest where my anger was.

And now what I feel is lonely.

Lonely and alone.

I wonder how long it takes the roots of one tree to reach another to send a message, and how far away my dad is, and how long it will take for my message to get to him. Probably too long. Probably it's all a silly story anyway.

Trees can't talk.

They can only listen.

Maybe they can't even do that.

Twenty-Four

A quiet shuffle of footsteps comes toward me. I peek down and see a familiar pair of green sneakers below the bathroom stall door.

"Hi, Maple," a tiny voice says. "Are you OK?"

I press my forehead against the door and feel Katy do the same.

"I'm having a rough time," I say. As soon as the words come out, more tears escape and drip down my face.

"I'm sorry," Katy says. "It's OK if you don't want to say what's going on. I know how that feels."

"Thanks." My nose drips, and I wipe it with the back of my hand. The cold metal of the door feels hard and more like a wall. Me on one side, Katy on the other. We're quiet for a minute.

"When my parents got divorced, I felt really alone," Katy says. "I didn't want to tell anyone about it. Not even my best friends. But I kind of wish I had now. Because maybe then I wouldn't have felt so lonely."

I remember when Katy's parents got divorced. Her mom fell in love with someone else and moved out of her house. Now Katy lives with just her dad, her older brother, and their cats.

"What else did it feel like?" I ask.

"Scary."

I nod, even though she can't see me.

"I was really mad, too. At my mom. And for a little while I blamed my dad. But then I realized that wasn't very fair of me. So then I felt guilty. Basically, I had a lot of emotions, and they were all pretty terrible. It was an awful time."

"I'm sorry," I say. "I wish I'd known. I would have tried to be a better friend."

"No, that's my point. I wish I'd told you. People can't help you if they don't know you're hurting inside."

The ache inside me stirs, as if it is agreeing. As if it wants me to open the door more, the wall between us, so Katy can put her hand on my chest and make the ache feel better.

I slowly turn the little metal knob on the door and open it.

"Hi," she says.

"Hi," I say.

She hugs me. Her hair smells like coconut.

"I'm still not ready to talk about it," I say.

She nods. "You don't have to. But when you're ready, I'm here. And so is Astrid."

"Thanks."

"We should go back to class before we get in trouble."

"OK."

"Hey," she says as we walk slowly down the hall. "Did you get another envelope in your locker today?"

I nod. "But I didn't have time to open it yet."

"It's from Oliver," she says. "He wants us to join his team."

"His team?"

"You know. His business!"

"Did he say what it is?"

"No. I guess we'll find out when we join. It's all top secret."

"Did Astrid get invited, too?"

"Yup. We're all supposed to go there after school tomorrow. What do you think?"

"If you two go, I'm definitely going."

"Perfect. We'll get a ride with my dad after school."

We pause at the door before we go inside.

Katy puts her hand on my shoulder. "You should take a deep breath before you go in, and then act like nothing happened. OK?"

I nod, and we both take a long deep breath together and let it out before she opens the door. I don't make eye contact with anyone when we go in. I just walk to my seat and listen to Ms. Kent explain how wonderful multiplication and division are.

"If you know that six times seven is forty-two," she says, all excited, "then you should quickly be able to remember that forty-two divided by seven is six! Do you see?"

We do see, because she has been telling us this all year.

I turn to look at Parker, who just kind of shrugs.

After school, Oliver runs over to me while I'm waiting in my bus line. He looks like he's going to hug me again! I don't think he has a crush on me, but I also don't know about this hugging thing. He drops his arms when I don't spread mine to hug back.

"Did you get my invitation?" he asks. He's wearing a dress shirt and tie, as if he just came from work.

"Yes!" I say. "Thanks!"

"So you're coming?"

I nod. "With Katy and Astrid. Should we bring anything?"

He looks thoughtful for a minute. "Just your imagination. I have some ideas for a logo I'd like to run by you. I could really use an artist on my team."

"An artist?" I say. I love to draw, but I don't think anyone has called me a real artist before.

He nods. "See you tomorrow, then!" He dashes away.

I turn to see if Astrid is in line yet and feel a tap on my shoulder.

"What on earth was that all about?" an ABC asks me.

I study him closely to figure out which one he is.

"You don't know who I am, do you?" he says.

"Errr."

He pulls his necklace out from under the neck of his shirt.

"Charlie!"

He smiles. "So was that top secret business stuff? Are you joining the team?"

I shrug. "I don't know about top secret, but he invited me over tomorrow."

"Hm. Interesting."

"Do you know what his business is?" I ask.

"No. I don't think anyone does."

"Except Carmella and Denzel. They must know."

"What kind of business can a fifth grader have?" Charlie asks.

"Beats me," I say. "But maybe it will be fun."

"My mom says we should enjoy being kids for as long as we can."

"I can see that. But if you don't like being a kid, why not skip to acting like a grown-up?"

"Capitalism," he says, shaking his head.

"Huh?"

"My mom also says capitalism is poisoning our generation."

"What does that mean?" I ask.

"I'm not totally sure. Something to do with being obsessed with making lots of money."

"Oh."

Our bus pulls up, and we get on and take our usual seats. I see Rory and Gabe in the way back. The bus picks up the high schoolers first, then the middle schoolers, so the older kids always get the best spots. Gabe is staring out the window ignoring everyone, and Rory is sitting with one of her friends. They look like they're having a serious conversation.

"Made it!" Astrid says, practically falling into our seat. "Oliver stopped me to make sure I was coming tomorrow. He sure is excited about it."

"Yeah," I say. "Do you think it's all a little weird?"

She shrugs. "I think it's a mystery. I won't know if it's weird until I find out what it is."

I nod. "Good point."

When we get to my stop, I jump up fast so I can get off the bus before Rory and Gabe. I race up the driveway and make it to the front door first. Ha! But when I turn around, they're both just walking slowly.

"Hey!" I say. "How come you're not racing?"

Neither of them answers.

"What's going on?"

They look at each other, then at me.

"You tell her," Gabe says.

"What?" I ask.

"Dad texted," Rory says.

"He did?" I'm not allowed to have my own phone yet, so I have to rely on Gabe and Rory for information. "What did he say?"

"C'mon, let's go out back."

Instead of going inside, we walk around the house and dump our backpacks by the tree, then walk down to the fence. We climb up and sit on top. Salt and Pepper come running over to us and honk. Rory sits on one side of me, Gabe on the other. Usually, I like sitting in the middle when we come out here. Like I'm in the middle of something fun about to happen. But today, I feel like I'm in the middle of a storm.

Rory takes out her phone and reads.

Hey, kids. Gonna spend some more time out here at Peter's cabin. Don't worry about me. Just need some Space Time, as you like to say. LOL. I love you all. Be good for Mom.

Gabe grunts. "I can't believe he said 'Be good for Mom.'"

"I can't believe he wrote 'LOL,'" Rory says.

"Is that all he wrote?" I ask. "Did he say when he's coming back?"

Rory hands me her phone so I can read the text myself. I notice that she and Gabe haven't replied.

"Text back and ask him when he's coming home!" I say, handing back the phone.

"Why bother?" Gabe says. "If he knew when he was coming home, he would say. He's just going to stay there as long as he wants. He doesn't care about us or Mom. All he cares about is himself."

"That's not true!" I'm so upset, I almost fall off the fence. Salt and Pepper run over, as if they were just waiting for me to be in reach so they can goose me. I'm tempted to push Gabe off so they can bite him instead.

"Then why else do you think he left us?" Gabe asks.

"He didn't leave us!"

"What else would you call it?" Rory asks.

"He just needs Space Time!"

"Stop being such a baby," Gabe says. "You know parents get divorced all the time."

"Who said they're getting divorced?" Rory asks.

"I'm just saying, it's the next logical step."

"You're wrong!" I say. "Give me your phone." I snatch it out of Rory's hand. She tries to grab it back, but I jump down and start running. Unfortunately, I am on the wrong side of the fence, and the Ganders come after me immediately. They peck at my legs, but I remember to stop moving, and when I do, they stop, too.

"Maple, get back here," Rory says.

"I'm calling Dad!"

I click on his name in her text and hit the call button. Salt and Pepper circle around me, as if they are waiting for me to put him on speaker phone so they can say hello.

After a few rings, a robot voice comes on and says the person's in-box is full. I try again and get the same thing. I try again.

"Maple, stop," Rory says.

"He's not going to answer!" Gabe jumps down on the other side of the fence and stomps off back toward the house.

I stand still, holding the phone.

"C'mon, Maple. Let's go get a snack or something."

I squeeze the phone but don't move. I just stare at my dad's last text.

I love you all. Be good for Mom.

"He said he loves us. But if that's true, why isn't he coming home?" My mouth starts to quiver like a baby's does before it starts to howl.

"I don't know," Rory says.

"What if we tell him we need him?" I start to text him.

Dad. Please come ho—

"Maple, stop. It won't make a difference."

"Yes, it will!"

Salt and Pepper start to waddle around my legs again.

"It won't," she says.

"How do you know!"

"Scroll up."

I look at her first. She is blurry through my own tears, but I can tell she's crying, too. Slowly, I swipe my thumb down the screen and read her and Gabe's group texts with my dad. The ache in my chest starts to feel like a piercing jab as I realize the truth. All the *Dad, please come home*'s aren't going to make a difference. After several of those from Gabe and Rory, he simply sent the same text about needing to be away for a little while and to be good for Mom.

If it was my phone, I'd chuck it as far as I could out into the meadow and let Salt and Pepper chase after it. But instead, I slowly walk over to Rory and hand it back.

I wipe my face with the back of my arm and climb over the fence. Salt and Pepper don't chase me. Rory follows me as I walk slowly back toward the house. I stop at the tree and climb on the tire swing. Even though she's too big, Rory climbs on the other side. Our knees press tightly against each other.

"He promised he'd make a tree fort with me," I say. "He *promised*."

"We'll just have to make it ourselves," Rory says. "How hard can it be?"

Hard, I want to say. Everything is hard. Too hard. I'm tired of everything feeling that way.

When I don't answer, Rory puts her hands over mine, and we hold the rope on the swing together. "We can make it," she says. "Gabe and Mom can help. It will be amazing, you'll see."

"But it was going to be something just Dad and I did. It was going to be our special project."

"Well, now it's going to be *our* special project. Besides, I'm way more fun." She squeezes my hands before she lets go. "You know I'm right!" she says, and jumps off the swing. "Now, c'mon! Let's go find your sketchbook so you can show me that drawing you made, and we can make a plan!"

I hesitate, then jump down. She puts her arm around me.

"We're going to make the best tree fort in the neighborhood," she says confidently. "I promise."

Twenty-Five

We have to take the bus to school in the morning because my mom can't be late for work again to bring us in. It's a bit weird sitting on the bus going toward school rather than away from it. Everything feels topsy-turvy. But for once, I arrive with Astrid before Katy, and we get to wait for her, just like they usually wait for me. It's already hot, so we stand in the shade of a tree.

"Are you excited to go to Oliver's today?" Astrid asks me. "We finally get to find out what his secret business is!"

"Oh no! I forgot to tell my mom!" I wish I had my own phone so I could text her now and tell her. Last night, we all barely talked again. My mom worked late, so Rory, Gabe, and I made a cereal smorgasbord for dinner, and when Mom came home, she said she needed a long bath, so we left her alone. Part of me was glad because I didn't want Gabe to tell her about Dad's text.

"We can ask Katy's dad to text her," Astrid says. "Come on! Let's get closer to the drop-off area so we can tell him when they get here before he drives off."

She skips down the sidewalk and I follow.

"Hi, girls!" Mr. Willis says when he pulls to the curb to drop off Katy. Astrid leans into the open passenger window as soon as Katy gets out and asks him to text my mom about going to Oliver's.

"Will do!" he says. "You doing OK, Maple?"

He gives me a look like my dog just died. Does he know about my dad? Would my mom have told him? They're pretty good friends, but this is private. I don't know why the idea bothers me, but it does.

"I'm fine," I say. "Thanks for texting my mom."

I know it's rude, but I turn around and start walking up the sidewalk toward school. Astrid and Katy follow, trying to grab my hands, but I don't let them.

"What's wrong?" Katy asks.

"Nothing!" I say in a way that makes it obvious something is. I march ahead.

Inside, Oliver is waiting for us at our lockers. He's wearing bright green dress pants, a white shirt, and a neon-blue tie. "Hi!" he says.

"Wow!" Astrid says. "You're awfully bright today!"

He grins. "My grandmother sent me these pants for my birthday. I think they have a lot of pizzazz."

"They sure do!" Katy says.

"You're all coming over today, right?"

We nod. Seeing Oliver looking so cheerful should brighten my mood, but instead it just makes me feel even more sour. He's always so happy. I guess I would be, too, if I had a perfect life like him. He's so smart, his secret business will probably make him a millionaire by the time he finishes middle school. Must be nice.

When we get to class, Ms. Kent is busy at the front of the room. I bet she's preparing to give us yet another quiz. This time, I'm going to concentrate. This time, I am going to PASS.

"Take a seat, everyone!" Ms. Kent says. "Settle down."

We all sit and wait for the big pep talk about how important division is.

I fidget with my pencil.

Ms. Kent clears her throat. "I have a surprise announcement to make," she says, standing up and holding her notebook that keeps track of our quiz results. "You've all been trying very hard all year to ace the division quiz. I know I've sounded like a broken record sometimes for telling you why I think this is so important—"

"That's for sure!" someone whispers behind me.

Ms. Kent goes on. "And I want all of you to know—*all* of you—that I am proud of you. You kept trying no matter what, and that's what counts. Every single one of you made a huge improvement. Absolutely *huge*! It's exactly what I was hoping for. And because of that, I'm declaring it: Party Time!"

We all look at one another, confused.

Ms. Kent bends down behind her big desk, reaching for something. Then she pulls out a large cooler that she heaves onto her desk. On top of the cooler is a shopping bag, from which she takes a bunch of paper bowls. "Who wants ice cream?" she asks.

The rest of the class cheers, but instead of being happy, I feel a wave of hot anger spread through my body. I don't want the last quiz I take this year to be the one I didn't finish! I want to prove I can do it again!

My dad told me that when he was a kid and full of emotion, he felt like a teakettle full of water coming to a boil that would whistle-scream angrily if you didn't take it off the burner. Whenever he got really upset, he'd make a noise just like he was a whistling teakettle, quietly at first, then louder and louder until everyone would stop and pay attention to him. I feel the whistle-scream in my chest just aching to burst out of me.

"Everyone, line up along the wall while I get this

set up," Ms. Kent says. "Oliver, can you help put out the toppings?"

Oliver skips to the front of the room and begins spreading out jars of toppings on the little table next to Ms. Kent's desk. Everyone hops up and goes to stand in line against the wall.

I get up slowly, still trying to keep my whistle-scream inside. Katy and Astrid line up next to me.

"This is great, huh?" Katy asks. "I bet Ms. Kent planned all along to give us a party no matter what, but she just wanted to see if we could ace the quiz anyway."

I nod, because I am afraid my anger will burst out of my mouth if I open it. "Mm-hmm," I say.

Parker gets in line behind me. "Hey, Maple! Isn't this amazing? No more quizzes *and* we get ice cream!"

"Mm-hmm," I say again.

"No more quizzes! No more timer!" Astrid says, elbowing me. "You must be so relieved!"

I nod, all out of *Mm-hmms*.

"You don't seem very excited," Katy says.

"Yeah," Astrid agrees. "What's wrong?"

"I have to go to the bathroom," I say. I turn and bump into Charlie.

"Sorry!" I say, letting some of my anger escape. I

push past him and walk-run out of the room as fast as I can without getting a hall pass. Again.

Ms. Kent must be too busy scooping ice cream to notice because she doesn't call after me. No one does.

I race down the hall toward the bathrooms, but instead of stopping, I just keep going. Down the hall, all the way to the front of the school. No one is around, which is surprising. I hear laughter burst from one of the classrooms nearby. A notice comes over the intercom reminding everyone there is an all-school assembly later. I walk straight to the door, push it open, and walk out.

The sun shines hot and bright on my face. I walk down the sidewalk, waiting for someone, anyone, to call after me. This is against school rules. This is not safe. This is *wrong*. But I keep walking. Faster and faster so that I'm almost running but not enough to be told not to, as if the crossing guard is going to come around the corner any minute and yell at me to slow down.

When I get to the corner where the school drive intersects with the main road, I am careful to look both ways, then I run across. And now that I'm running and no longer on school property, I sprint.

Twenty-Six

"Maple! Maple! Wait up!!!"

I turn to see Charlie running toward me. I stop and let him catch up.

"What are you doing?" he asks. "You're going to get in trouble!"

"So are you! And why did you come after me? You're missing the party!"

"I was worried about you," he says. His cheeks are bright red and shiny from running on this hot morning. "Why did you take off?"

"Did Ms. Kent notice?"

"I don't think so. I don't think anyone really noticed. Sorry."

I shrug. "I don't blame them. I'm sure they care more about the ice cream."

"I don't."

I feel my own cheeks get hot, and I bet they're bright red, too.

"Thanks," I say. "But you should probably go back. Maybe you could sneak in, and no one would notice."

"Maybe we both should. What did you run off for, anyway? Were you mad about the party?"

I start to say no, but then a little "Mm-hmm" escapes me.

"How come?"

"I just . . . I finally figured out how to pass the quiz, and now I won't get a chance to ace it again like everyone else. I feel like Ms. Kent gave up on me. And Parker, too."

"Oh. Yeah. I see your point. I think. But I bet she was just trying to be nice." He reaches for the labyrinth pendant on his neck and traces the path with his thumb as he puzzles this all out. I wish I had something like that to help me think and find answers, too. But no little pendant can find the kind of answers I need. Like how to get my dad to come home and stop being so mad at my mom all the time. Dadlandia feels so real now. As if he really is there, and he's never going to want to leave and come back to us.

"Are you OK, Maple? You seem really quiet and sad lately."

I don't know how to answer without starting to cry, and I definitely do not want to cry in front of Charlie. Or anyone. But for some reason, the truth jumps out of me.

"My dad left us," I say.

The words sound so awful and real when I say them out loud. I can't believe I'm telling this secret to an ABC and not to Astrid or Katy.

"He said he needed space. But what he really means is he needed to get away from my mom. And I'm afraid he's never coming back and that my parents are going to get divorced. My dad promised he'd spend time with me this summer building a tree fort, and now he isn't going to, even though it's almost my birthday, and I don't think he even loves us anymore. And my mom is so sad and I think she secretly cries all the time, and I don't know how to make her feel better, and my brother Gabe is really angry and he won't talk to us, and Rory's acting like nothing is wrong, and everything is just so, so terrible, but no one knows, so they just expect me to be normal, but I can't be because I can't stop thinking about all these things all the time and . . ." I stop to take a breath.

Charlie's eyes get bigger and bigger the more words gush out of me. It's the most I've ever told anyone, and it feels like teakettle-me just let out all the steam that was waiting to whistle-scream. But I still don't cry. In fact, I feel kind of relieved in some strange way.

Charlie reaches up and puts his hand on my shoulder, as if he thinks I might topple over from letting go of the weight of everything I just said. It's something Rory would do.

"Sorry," I say. "I probably shouldn't have told you all that."

"It's OK," he says. "That's what friends are for."

Friends?

He takes his hand back, as if reading my mind.

But I realize, we are friends. We are now.

"Thanks for listening," I say.

We stand there for a minute. It feels a little awkward. Then Charlie kind of clears his throat.

"So I guess you weren't really upset about the quiz, then, huh?"

He looks so serious about pointing out something that is suddenly so obvious, I can't help it. I start laughing. I give him a gentle shove, and he shoves me back.

"Should we try to sneak back into school so we don't get in trouble?" Charlie asks.

"Do you think we can?"

He shrugs.

I realize if we get caught, we are both going to be in BIG trouble. As soon as someone notices we're missing, they'll call our parents. Maybe even the police! And then my mom will be really worried. What was I thinking?

"Let's try," I say. "Fast!"

We race back to the school and creep up the walkway. It's still first period, but we notice a car pulling up to drop someone off late.

"Now's our chance!" Charlie says. He grabs my hand, and we dash up the path to the school, just like in the movies.

I smile, thinking how Astrid and Katy would laugh if they saw us and say, "See! We told you!"

When we catch up to the kid and her parent going in, we act casual and walk behind them.

"Are you two late?" the parent asks.

"Oh, no, we forgot something outside, so our teacher said we could run and get it."

"What was it?" the parent asks.

"Uh . . ." Charlie begins.

"His necklace!" I say. "It fell off and it's really special, so our teacher let us come look for it."

Charlie nods.

I cannot believe Charlie and I both just told such a big lie. But the parent seems to believe us because they hold the door open for us and we slip in.

We fast-walk down the hall to Ms. Kent's room. We can hear the party still going on from out in the hallway. People sure do get excited about ice cream.

"That was a big lie," Charlie says.

"Sorry. I don't usually do that."

"It's OK, I think," Charlie says. "Since it didn't hurt anyone."

I nod. Charlie has definitely changed. Or maybe I just never really knew him.

"I'll slip in first and cause a distraction, then you slip in," he says.

"OK." I wait until I hear a little commotion and then quickly duck inside. Charlie is in front of the room already, leading the class in a "We want seconds!" chant.

No one notices me, so I quietly join the chorus. Charlie sees me and smiles. My stomach does a funny little flip-flop.

"Where were you?" Astrid asks, coming up behind me. She has chocolate in the corners of her mouth.

"Oh, nowhere," I say. "I just had to go to the bathroom." Another lie. I try to use Charlie's excuse of it not hurting anyone to make me feel better. It only kind of works.

"With Charlie?"

"No!" I say. "We just happened to need to go at the same time."

She gives me a look that says she definitely does not believe me.

"Well, you better hurry up and get some ice cream before it runs out."

"I'm not really hungry," I say.

"Now I *know* you're lying," Astrid says. She gives me a little push toward the ice cream line. "The rainbow sprinkles are the best," she tells me. "Hurry up!"

Twenty-Seven

"You're all here because I think you have a special talent and would be a strong asset to the team," Oliver says.

We're sitting in a circle on the grass in his backyard. Me, Astrid, Katy, Denzel, and Carmella. Oliver has changed from his school outfit. Now he's wearing a green short-sleeved button-up shirt with turtles on it. His tie is purple. He dresses like a businessman, but in a loud and bright way.

"I'd like to give a warm welcome to our new members. Team, meet Maple, Katy, and Astrid." He says this as if we haven't all known one another since kindergarten.

Carmella and Denzel nod at us professionally.

Katy giggles. Astrid elbows her to shush.

"Our first order of business is our nondisclosure agreement. In order to join the team officially, you three need to promise you will not share what you learn today with anyone outside the team. Please raise your right hands."

We look at each other. This feels weird.

"What does *nondisclosure* mean?" Katy asks.

"I just told you," Oliver says. "It's a business thing." He raises his hand. "Repeat after me. I solemnly swear I will not share the secrets of the business I am about to learn."

We repeat his words.

"Perfect. Now, let's head up to the office."

Oliver's tree house is a lot like Astrid's clubhouse, only it's up in the branches and has a perfect ladder leading up to it. Inside, there is a small table and a filing cabinet with one drawer, a dry-erase board on one wall, and a tiny desk. Everything is little so it can all fit, but because everything else is small, I feel big. Almost too big. We look like giants as we squeeze in around the table in the middle of the room. There aren't any chairs, so we sit cross-legged, our knees pressed against one another. Oliver closes the curtains in the two windows of the house, then joins us at the crowded table. He clears his throat.

"Thank you for coming today," he says. "I hope you'll excuse the appearance, but I only recently moved my office here for the summer."

"Seems pretty perfect to me," I say. I hear the jealousy in my voice and feel guilty.

"Thank you. Now, this is a very important moment for my business, and what I'm about to reveal will hopefully be the launch of a thriving entrepreneurial venture someday."

Astrid raises her hand.

"Please hold your questions until the end of my presentation," Oliver says. "As I was saying, it's an important day." He nods to Carmella, who crawls over to the file cabinet, opens a drawer, and pulls out a multicolored flower made with tissue paper attached to a hot-pink pipe cleaner.

"Behold!" Oliver says. "My business model."

We stare.

"It's . . . a paper flower?" Astrid asks.

"A *rainbow* flower!" Oliver replies. "The theme of my business: Rainbow Blossoms Unlimited."

"I don't understand," Katy says.

"Rainbows are the symbol of love and hope," Oliver

explains. "They are also rare and beautiful! Denzel helped me create this prototype. I'm hoping Maple can create an advertising logo, since she's the best artist I know."

I feel my cheeks blush a little.

"Our mission at Rainbow Blossoms Unlimited is to create a product that will make people appreciate the joy that bright colors bring to the world." He takes the flower from Carmella and tucks it through the buttonhole on the front pocket of his shirt. "They can serve many functions, as you'll see. For example, a boutonniere, like this. Or"—he motions to Carmella, and she pulls another flower from the drawer, then wraps it around her wrist to make a big bracelet—"a corsage!"

Oliver joins Carmella at the cabinet and pulls out a box of pipe cleaners and some rainbow tissue, then carefully demonstrates how to make a flower before we all give it a try.

"How much are you going to charge for these things?" Astrid asks, trying to fold a piece of paper just so.

"Oh, uhhhh." Oliver hesitates, looking a little taken off guard. "I mean . . ." He glances over at Carmella and Denzel.

"It's just for fun," Carmella says.

Astrid scrunches her face. "What do you mean?"

"We-ell," Oliver says. "For now, this is . . . you

know . . ." But he doesn't finish. Instead, he looks nervously at Carmella and Denzel again.

"It's pretend," Denzel says. "The business."

"Only for now," Oliver adds. "I like to think of this as an internship."

"A what?" Katy asks.

"It's something you do to learn a trade. An internship, I mean."

"So we're just supposed to pretend to be part of your business?" Astrid asks, all serious.

"If you don't want to play, that's fine," Oliver says. His voice sounds funny, like he's about to cry. "But please remember you signed a nondisclosure agreement, so you can't tell anyone about this!"

Astrid, Katy, and I look at one another. This is *not* what we were expecting. It's all *make-believe*? But Oliver seems so serious!

Astrid starts to wrap a pipe cleaner around her folded paper. "I'll play," she says. "Why not?"

"Me too," Katy says. "Your secret is safe with us. Right, Maple?"

I realize that my mouth has dropped open. Am I the only one who is shocked? Oliver's super-secret business was all just *pretend*? A giggle escapes me. Then another. Soon I am laughing so hard, I cannot stop. But I quickly realize no one else thinks this is funny. In fact, they're all staring at me.

"Are you laughing at me, Maple?" Oliver asks.

"N-no," I say.

"Then what's so funny?"

I look at Astrid and Katy for help, but they seem as shocked that I laughed as I am that this is all just a game. "I just . . . You were so serious, I thought it was real." I laugh nervously, which I know right away is a big mistake.

"Wow," Oliver says. "Of the three of you, I thought you were the least likely to make fun of me. No offense, Katy and Astrid."

"What? No! I—"

"You should go," he interrupts. "I hope you'll respect my privacy and not tell anyone about my business. Which *will* be real. Someday."

"I'm sorry!" I say. "I didn't mean to hurt your feelings! I want to stay and play. I was just surprised, that's all! You seem so serious all the time. I just assumed this was . . . that . . ." Ugh. I guess I really don't know what to say. I wish Katy and Astrid would do something to help.

Oliver takes a deep breath. "There's nothing wrong with being serious."

"I know!" I say. "I know that. I really do. I'm sorry. I misunderstood, that's all."

"Maple isn't mean," Astrid says. "I think you just surprised her."

Finally. I turn to Katy to see if she'll agree. She nods.

"Fine," Oliver says, pushing more supplies toward me.

A wave of relief passes over me, but of course now it feels awkward. I take the paper and quietly try to make a flower, hoping someone changes the subject.

"You know what would be cool?" Carmella asks. "T-shirts with a picture of our flowers. Once the business is real, I mean. We could wear them to advertise."

"Yeah!" says Denzel.

"I bet Maple could design a shirt," Katy says. "She's the best artist *I* know, too."

"Thanks," I say, finishing up my first flower. Usually that compliment would make me feel all warm and happy inside, but I think she said it just to be nice because she can tell how bad I feel about hurting Oliver's feelings. I'm starting to feel like I don't belong here. Everyone is so nice and perfect, and I'm not.

I'd say this is the worst day ever, but that happened the day my dad told us he wasn't coming home. I guess that just makes this the worst *week* ever. Lucky me.

Twenty-Eight

When Katy's dad drops me off that night, the first thing I notice is how different our house feels from Oliver's perfect one. After our "meeting," Oliver's dad made pizza on the grill, and we got to choose our own toppings. Every time his parents were near each other, they would touch somehow. They were like magnets. When they got close, *whomp*, they pushed together and stuck. My mom and dad are never like that anymore, except for that brief time at the concert, when they snuggled on the picnic blanket. Mostly, I think my dad is the opposite. Every time he gets close to us, *whoosh*, something pushes him away.

• • •

I wander through our quiet house, looking for my family. No one in the kitchen. No one in the dining room. It's dusk now, and the house feels dark and a little scary. As soon as I turn a light on, though, I hear my mom.

"Maple! We're outside!" she calls through the open window overlooking the backyard.

I follow her voice and find Gabe, Rory, and my mom standing around a big pile of boards, all spread out on the lawn. My boards. My tree-fort boards.

"What are you doing?" I ask.

"What does it look like?" Rory says. "Planning out how to help you make your tree fort."

"You started without me? Dad's supposed to be the one who—"

"You know Dad's not going to help," Gabe says, all cold. "It's just us."

"He can always help when he comes back," my mom says, giving Gabe a look. "We wanted to see how many materials Dad collected, honey. To make sure we had enough to get a good start. We thought it would be a fun birthday treat to all work on this with you. Maybe we can finish in time for your birthday, and you can have your friends over for a grand opening!"

"That's two weeks away." When I say the words, I realize two weeks sounds really close when trying to plan on building an entire tree fort, but it feels miles away when they are saying my dad won't be home by then. Two whole weeks? We've never been apart this long. Not ever.

My mom seems to see me realize this. She drops the board she's holding and walks over to hug me.

"It's not forever, Maple," she tells me. "He'll be back."

Gabe moves some of the bigger boards around to make a square. "This could be the frame for the platform. If we put this together first and attach it to the tree, then we could hoist that piece of plywood up and attach it to the frame. That would make a sturdy floor."

Rory looks up at the tree, squinting. "We need to make a ladder," she says. "It's gonna be tricky getting all these pieces up there, and Dad's stepladder isn't tall enough."

My mom lets go of me and points to a pile of wood scraps. "We could hammer these up the trunk for footing," she says. "If we measure the floor pieces out first, we can place them on those three low branches, then adjust as we go, using the level to make sure we have an even floor. What do you think, Maple?"

I look up at my tree, which is all shadows in the fading light. It seems impossible, that's what I think. There's no way we can make something that looks anything like the tree fort in my sketchbook. And there's definitely no way it's going to look anything like Oliver's fancy one. I bet his parents hired professionals to make his. It has *real windows*. Astrid's clubhouse came as a kit. But mine . . . I look at the mismatched pieces of wood all spread out in the overgrown grass. Some boards my dad bought on sale last year, when he was supposed to make my fort. Others are leftover scraps from odd jobs he's done over the years and things he's scavenged from "Free" piles neighbors leave at the end of their driveways when they've finished their own projects.

The pile makes me feel hopeless. We'll never get a tree fort out of all this junk.

And jealous. My tree fort will never look like Oliver's.

And angry. My dad doesn't even care that he broke his promise. Again.

And guilty. My mom, Rory, and Gabe are trying really hard to do something nice for me, and I should be grateful.

"Maple," my mom says. "We can do this without Dad. He's not the only one who knows how to use a hammer and a circular saw, ya know."

"Yeah!" Rory says. "It's going to be so much fun! I can't wait to use the saw!"

"Uh, let's leave the saw to me," my mom says. She looks at each of us, as if already imagining what we might do with a saw if she wasn't around. "No one, and I mean *no one*, uses any tools or even works on this project when I'm not home. Got it?"

"We'll be careful!" Gabe says. "We're not children!"

"Maple is definitely a child," Rory says. "And technically, we are not adults yet. You have to be eighteen."

"I just meant we're not little kids," Gabe says. "We don't need Dad around to help. We can do this on our own."

"You can do it with me," my mom says. "No discussion. If you show me how responsible you can be, I'll teach you how to use the saw. But it can be dangerous. It's not a toy."

"Yes!" Rory says.

"It's getting late," my mom says. "What do you think, Maple? Does it look like we have enough material here to make the kind of tree fort you want?"

I picture the drawing I made in my sketchbook again, then look at the piles of wood scraps. There's not nearly enough to make my dream fort. It probably wouldn't even be enough to make one side of Oliver's fancy one. But I nod quietly. Looking at my mom, Gabe, and Rory, I realize maybe we're a *little* like magnets, in our own way. We find ways to stick together. We always do, even when we annoy each other. I just wish I understood why we seem to push my dad away.

"It will be fine," I say. "Thanks."

"Great!" she says. "Well, I guess we know what we're doing this weekend!"

We pile all the wood by size next to the tree, then go inside to get ready for bed.

In my closet, I open my sketchbook and look at my dream tree fort one last time.

Twenty-Nine

One week later, on the last day of school, my mom tells us she'll drive us in as a treat. Usually, my dad makes us a last-day-of-school celebratory breakfast. Then, on the drive in, he sings songs he made up about summer and all the fun things we'll do. I realize now we hardly ever end up doing any of them for one reason or another. Mostly because they're all too silly, but also because my dad never gets around to it.

I can't believe another whole week has gone by and he still isn't home. All he could bother to do was send Gabe and Rory other "I'm taking a few more days" and "Be good for your mom" texts.

"Eighth grade is finally in sight!" Rory says. "Next year I will be queen of middle school."

"Enjoy it while you can," Gabe says. "Because once you get to high school, it's the end of the world as you know it."

"Gabe!" my mom says. "What a terrible thing to say!"

"I'm just telling the truth! Middle school is socially hard, and high school is academically and socially hard. Unless you don't care about your grades. Then it doesn't matter."

My mom shakes her head.

"It won't feel like the end of the world to me!" Rory says. "I like academics. Mostly." She's quiet for a minute, looking out the window. "If it really was the end of the world, what would you do before the actual end?"

"Who are you asking?" I say.

"All of you."

"Hug you," my mom says. "I'd hold you all as tight as I could."

"I'd probably fart," Rory says. "I don't want my body to have any gas in it when I'm dead."

"I'd go to the bathroom," Gabe says. "Did you know that when you die, anything that was in you leaks out?"

"Gross!" I say. "Really?"

"*This* is what you'll be thinking about when you have ten minutes left on earth?" my mom asks. "Pooping and farting?"

"Why do people think farts are gross?" Rory says. "Everyone does it."

"Because they stink!" I say. "Obviously."

"So do babies, but people think they're cute," Rory says.

"Rory!" my mom says. "Honestly, sometimes I don't know where you come up with these thoughts!"

"I'm just stating the truth!"

"Babies smell wonderful," my mom says. "Most of the time. Oh, I miss when you were babies. You were all so cute and sweet."

"What did we smell like?" I ask.

I can see my mom smiling in the rearview mirror. "You each had your own distinct smell," she says.

"What was mine?" Gabe asks.

"Carrots!" my mom says. "Sweet and earthy." She reaches over and fluffs his hair. "You could not get enough of mashed carrots when you first started eating solids. Your father would joke that your hair would turn orange."

At the mention of Dad, she frowns a little. "And Rory

smelled like diaper cream." She turns back to wink at Rory. "And baby powder. It was a *nice* smell."

Rory rolls her eyes.

"What about me?" I ask.

My mom catches my eye in the mirror again. "Hmmm. You're hard to remember, Maple, I was so busy chasing Gabe and Rory around. They didn't give me a lot of chances to just sit and hold you and smell you."

"The third child is always ignored," I say. "That's what Dad said." He was the third child in his family, too. He told me he was always overlooked and forgotten because his two older sisters were so loud and bossy and needed attention.

"Not true!" my mom says. "You were just my easy child. You were always content to sit in your high chair and watch your brother and sister."

"Sounds boring," I say.

"Hey!" Rory smacks me playfully.

"Cheerios," my mom finally says. "That's the first solid food you fed yourself, and you loved them. You always had Cheerio breath."

"See?" Rory says. "Stinky."

"Cheerios aren't stinky!"

"Oat-y, then. I bet you smelled like the donkeys."

"Hey!" I smack her back, a little less playfully.

"It was a wonderful smell," my mom says. "Like I said. All babies smell beautiful."

Rory sticks her head out the window and howls like a dog.

"What on earth?" my mom asks.

"Arhoooo!"

When we pull to the curb, my mom reaches back for my hand. "I love you very much. Enjoy your last day."

"Oh no!" I say, remembering we didn't pack a special lunch.

"What is it?"

"We forgot our last-day-of-school lunch!"

"What do you mean?"

"Dad always makes us something special," Rory says. "Instead of school lunch, he lets us bring a treat from Jesse's."

"He didn't text to tell you?" Gabe asks. "How shocking."

My mom sighs. "I'm sorry, kids. I'm doing my best."

"It's not *your* fault," Gabe says. "It's Dad's. Once again, he let us down."

"Gabe, please," my mom says.

"Crap on a cupcake!" Rory yells. "I could've gone back to Jesse's!"

I bet she's upset about that only because she missed a chance to see Jesse.

"Mom, is it too late?" I ask. "Could we go get something now?"

"Yeah!" Rory says. "Who cares if we're a little late for school."

"But I'd be even more late for work than I already am!"

"They'll understand," Rory says. "Tell them you did it for your precious children!"

"Pleeeeeeease!" I say.

My mom makes a face like my dad sometimes does before he gets up to mischief. It makes me miss him. My heart feels heavy in my chest.

"You know what? Fine!" my mom says. She puts the blinker on and pulls out of the drop-off lane.

"Arhoooo!" Rory yells again as we leave the parking lot and turn onto the main road.

Gabe doesn't say a word. He hardly ever does anymore. It seems like he's angry all the time. Watching him makes me feel angry, too. My dad being gone is hurting everyone in different ways. Doesn't he realize that? Doesn't he care?

I think about my mom's answer about the end of the world. She didn't have to even think about it. She'd hug us tight. I wonder what my dad would say. I wonder if we would be the first thing he'd think of. But I guess I'll never know. Because he's not even here to ask. He's probably off in Dadlandia having the time of his life.

Thirty

At school, Ms. Kent lets us play a math game that's like the show *Jeopardy!* only with numbers, and it's really fun. Then, at the end of the day, Oliver gathers our team together to tell us how much he appreciates us and hopes to hold lots of meetings over the summer. I tell him for the hundredth time how sorry I am that I hurt his feelings, and he just shrugs, which is why I keep feeling like I need to apologize. I bet he'll never try to hug me again. Instead of being relieved, I just feel bad.

Katy rides the bus with me and Astrid after school because they both agreed to come for a sleepover and to help with the tree fort tomorrow. We squeeze together on one seat on the bus. The ABC's and Dora sit in their usual spots nearby. As soon as they overhear us talking about the fort, they ask if they can come help, too. Charlie looks the most excited. Astrid says it's because he has a crush on me, but I think it's just because he's nice and wants to be friends.

"Can I come, too?" Dora asks.

"You're too little," Bryce tells her.

"No, I'm not!" Dora says. "I'm a good helper."

"You don't have to do everything we do," Adam tells her.

"I know that! I just want to have fun."

"You can come," I say. "We'll need lots of help."

"Yay!"

At my stop, we skip up the driveway. Rory and Gabe both went to spend the night at friends' houses, so it's just the three of us.

"Let's go say hi to the Ganders," I say. I run inside to get us a snack, then Katy and Astrid follow me out back and we race to the fence. The minute Salt and Pepper see us, they come charging toward the fence, honking wildly. We climb the fence, and I hand Astrid and Katy each a few crackers.

"We're not supposed to feed them after the Rory

incident," I remind them. "But if you drop a few crumbs, it'll be OK."

We watch them happily scramble in the grass any time a crumb "drops."

"Geese are funny," Katy says. "I wonder what it's like not to have fingers or toes."

"I wonder what it's like to have a beak instead of a mouth," Astrid says.

I picture how I would draw Katy and Astrid as geese and giggle to myself.

"I'm glad I'm not a goose," I say. "It would be awful not to be able to draw."

"You could hold a pen in your beak!" Astrid says.

"Oooh, like that famous elephant who painted with its trunk!" Katy says.

"I've never tried to write with my mouth," I say.

Astrid finishes her last cracker and wipes her hands free of crumbs over the Ganders. "I bet it would be harder with a beak."

We watch the geese for a bit longer, then decide to go look at the lumber for the tree fort.

"How did you make a platform way up there?" Astrid asks, shading her eyes from the sun with her hand.

We all look up at the first set of branches on the tree.

"A little ingenuity," I say, proud of my Astrid-like word. "Gabe and Rory and my mom did most of it. My dad was supposed to help me with the hard parts, but . . ."

"But what?" Astrid asks.

I look over at Katy.

"You can tell us," she says. "If you're ready."

Astrid nods.

"I don't really want to talk about it," I say.

"You don't have to if you don't want to," Astrid says. "But is everything OK? Things seemed a little weird with your mom and dad the last time I was over."

I nod, even though things are not OK. Definitely not. Did he really stop loving my mom? But why? She's the best in the world. If he just needed a little break, why hasn't he come back yet? What if something happened to him and *that's* why he hasn't come home? Would my mom even know? He never answers his phone when she tries to reach him. How would she know if something happened? It's been days since he texted Rory and Gabe. What if he went out on the lake at his friend's cabin and his boat tipped over? What if he went swimming and had a heart attack? What if . . .

"Maple! Are you OK?" Katy puts her hand on my shoulder. "You look a little pale all of a sudden."

I take a deep breath.

What if all this time I've been thinking about Dad happily stuck in Dadlandia, he's been stuck somewhere else? Somewhere real? What if he actually wants to come home? Suddenly, I feel like I might throw up.

"I don't feel so good," I say.

We walk over to a sunny spot in the grass and sit down.

"Sometimes it does help to talk about it," Astrid says. "You know what they say? Let it all out?"

Katy smiles knowingly at me.

I take a deep breath. "My dad left."

I take another deep breath.

"He and my mom haven't been getting along lately. He went to his friend's cabin to take a 'break.' At first, we thought he'd only be gone a few days. But that turned into two weeks. And now we don't know when he's coming back."

"Oh no!" Katy says. "That's awful!"

It doesn't feel good to hear her say that. But at least it feels true. For a long time now, my family doesn't seem to want to say the truth out loud. That this is awful.

"Are you all right?" Astrid asks. "I can't imagine how you must feel."

"It feels awful," I tell her. "Katy already described it perfectly."

"I think when people say 'Let it all out,' they mean it's OK to cry," Katy says, bringing us back to the subject. "Do you want to cry, Maple?"

"No!" I say. "I don't want to cry. I want to scream!"

"That works, too."

"Yes!" Astrid says. "It's OK to be angry. You have every right! Scream, Maple! Scream!"

They look at me expectantly. I open my mouth, but I don't know what to do. "What do I scream?"

"Anything!" Katy says. "Just make a noise!"

"Yes!" Astrid says. "Howl like an angry dog!"

I make an uneasy face at them.

"You can do it," Katy says. "You'll feel better!"

"We can all do it together!" Astrid says. "On the count of three!"

"One," Katy says.

"Two," Astrid adds.

"Three?" I say.

We all breathe in at the same time, then yell out, "Arhoooo!"

"That wasn't very loud," Katy points out. "Do you feel better?"

I shake my head.

"Again!" Astrid says.

We count again, and this time we scream even louder, "Arrrrhoooooo!!!"

"That seemed better," Katy says. "Well?"

I shake my head again.

"Keep trying," Astrid says. "And I mean really as loud as we can!"

We count again and breathe in together and then really let it all out. "ARRRRHOOOOOO!!!" we scream. I try so hard, the back of my throat hurts.

In the distance, a dog barks, then another. Soon it seems every dog in the neighborhood is barking. The donkeys bray and the Ganders start honking. We all look at one another, shocked. Then we burst out laughing. Once I start, I cannot stop. I laugh so hard, my stomach hurts. Katy falls backward on the grass.

"Something came out my nose!" Astrid says. Then we all laugh harder.

She wipes her nose and looks at something on the tip of her finger. "I think it was a cracker."

That does it. I am laughing so hard, tears stream down my face. Katy howls.

We're so loud, we don't hear my mom until the screen door creaks open and slams shut behind her as she comes outside.

"Wow, girls," she says. "I clearly missed a good one. What was all that racket?"

When I can finally stop laughing, I sit up and wipe my eyes. "When did you get home?" I ask. "Did you get out of work early?"

"Yup!" she says. "My boss sent me home early, since she knows it's the last day of school and I'd want to get home to celebrate with you. I thought we could get a head start on the walls." She looks high above at the platform we managed to put up this past week.

First, we made the ladder like she suggested. I was afraid the nails would hurt the tree and felt discouraged, but Rory googled it and said the tree would be fine. Then we handed up the best boards to Gabe to make a frame for the floor. He used a level to make them straight and to adjust them on the branches. Then Rory, Gabe, and I positioned ourselves on the frame while my mom handed us squares of plywood to hammer onto it. They were random small scraps we found, so we had to fit them together like a big jigsaw puzzle, but we managed to get a floor all set. Now it's time to make the sides.

"I'll go get the toolbox!" I say.

When I come back, Astrid, Katy, and my mom have started to make a new pile of wood we can use for the walls.

"You know," my mom says, "I think maybe we should

wait until tomorrow so Rory and Gabe can help. This really is a family project. They might be upset if we work on it without them."

"It's not really a family project," I say. "Because Dad isn't here."

I don't know why I had to say that. I can tell my words hurt my mom.

Astrid and Katy look uncomfortable.

"Sorry," I say. "I didn't mean it."

My mom bites her lower lip as if she's trying not to cry.

"I'm really sorry, Mom! I promise."

I run over to hug her. My chest hurts, knowing I hurt her. How could I say something so insensitive?

"It's all right," she says.

"No, it's not! It was a terrible thing to say." I squeeze her as hard as I can.

"I know you're angry," she says. "And you have every right to be."

"I'm not angry at you, though, Mom! I didn't mean it!"

"It's OK, Maple. I promise." She hugs me back tightly.

I pull away from her and look into her eyes.

"I heard you howl," she says. "What was that all about?"

I glance over at Astrid and Katy.

"We were trying to let it all out," I say.

"Let what out?"

"Our anger."

She nods. "Did it work?"

"I think so. We upset all the neighborhood dogs, though."

"I noticed. You caused quite a commotion."

"Want to do it with us?" Astrid asks.

"Yeah!" Katy says. "You should!"

"Hmm," my mom says, putting her hands on her hips. "I'm not sure I want to upset all the dogs again."

"Aw, they were just joining in!" I say.

"All right. Why not?"

"On the count of three," I say. "Gather up all the anger you have inside and get ready to let it out!"

We all look at my mom. She smiles and takes a really deep breath. "Ready."

I count down and we all let out the loudest *arhoooo* yet. As soon as we stop, we listen for the dogs, who all return the howling. The donkeys and geese, too. But this time, instead of cracking up, we all just smile at one another in a knowing way. It does feel good to let it all out. It feels great.

The next day, we get to work on the tree fort as soon as Gabe and Rory come home. The ABC's show up with a toolbox and everything. My mom shows us how to measure the boards and mark them just so, and we spend the morning getting them ready for the circular saw, which the ABC's are very excited about until my mom tells them she's the only one going near it. She has Gabe hold each board steady over the sawhorses while she carefully cuts along the lines we made. Then we take turns climbing up the makeshift ladder and start to hammer the sides. It is a lot harder than any of us thought, but pretty soon we have one side up, then another. We leave a small hole in one corner of the floor to squeeze up through. We couldn't figure out how to make a roof, so the tree fort looks more like a lookout tower, with the sides only as tall as our waists. We leave one side fully open so we can sit on the floor and look out at the neighbor's property and watch the Ganders and the donkeys. Katy started calling the donkeys the Brays, which we all think is a perfect name.

When everyone goes home, I get my sketchbook and climb up in the fort. I look out at the view and listen to the leaves gently rustle all around me. I wish my dad was here. I bet he'd like being in the fort, enjoying the view. But part of me doesn't wish he was here. Why should he get to enjoy it when he left us and we had to do all the work without him? That seems a bit harsh. But it also feels a bit true.

Thirty-One

On the morning of my birthday, I wake up and find a brand-new sketchbook outside my door with a note from my mom: "A little present to start your new year with," it says. "I hope eleven is your best one yet."

Every year, my mom gives me a new sketchbook like this, and every year, she says she hopes it's my best one yet. I take the book back to bed with me and touch the cover before I open it, as if I can feel the new comics waiting to be made inside.

I grab my pencil case and pull out a Sharpie, then open to the first page.

Suddenly there's a clanging sound outside my door. I slowly push it open to find Gabe and Rory banging on metal pots with wooden spoons from the kitchen.

"It's your birthday! Happy birthday! It's your birthday! Time to par-tay!" They do a ridiculous dance as they sing their made-up song.

My dad always writes a special birthday song about us that includes fun memories of things that happened over the year. On the morning of our birthday, he wakes us up and sings to us, getting us all excited for our big day. I know Rory and Gabe are doing their best to make up for my dad not being here, but it's just not the same. I smile, though, to show them I appreciate their efforts.

Rory grabs my arm to pull me out of my closet, then leads me downstairs to the dining room. They've decorated with streamers and put a crown on the plate at the head of the table where my dad usually sits.

"Take the seat of honor and don your crown, my lady!" Rory says.

My mom walks out with a big tray stacked with pancakes with two number one candles to make an eleven. They sing "Happy Birthday" to me and then wait for me to make a wish.

"Make it a good one!" Gabe says.

I take a deep breath and squeeze my eyes shut.

I pause.

I haven't thought of what to wish for. What do I want?

"Hurry up!" Rory says. "Or the wax will melt on the pancakes."

The first thing that comes to mind is Dad. He should be here. He's never missed my birthday. I should make a wish for him to come home. For everything to go back to the way it was. But for some reason, instead, I silently say to myself, *Happiness*, and blow out the candles.

They all clap and take their seats, and we dig in.

"Can Maple open our presents now?" Rory asks through a mouthful of pancake. A bit of syrup dribbles down her chin.

"It's up to her!" my mom says.

"Now!" Rory says. "Then you can spend the day using them!"

I nod. "But let's finish eating. Cold pancakes are yucky."

As soon as we finish, Gabe clears our plates while Rory brings the presents to me. There's something from each of them in different-colored gift bags.

I like presents but don't love opening them in front of people because I'm afraid if I don't like what they got me, they might be able to tell. But I always love what my family gives me. It's not the same without my dad here, though. He likes to make a big show of placing the presents in front of us and making silly guesses of what they could be.

"Mine first!" says Gabe. "The purple."

I start with the handmade card taped to the outside of the bag. Inside is a drawing of the Ganders wearing party hats with a combined speech bubble that says, "Take a gander at this, Maple! If you don't like it, we'll goose ya!"

"Good one," I say.

I carefully remove the tissue paper sticking out the top of the bag and reach inside. It's a beautiful set of new Sharpies.

"The Ultimate Collection!" Gabe says. "Do you like it?"

"Forty-five colors!" I say. "Wow!" I jump up and give him a hug.

"Not so tight!" he yells. "Sheesh!" But he squeezes me back just as tightly. I can tell it's his way of letting me know he loves me.

"Me next!" Rory says, pushing her blue gift bag toward me.

I pull out a box of watercolor markers. I've heard of them but never used them before.

"I thought they would be fun to try," Rory says. "To change things up a little! The packaging shows all the different ways you can use them. Do you like them? You can return them for something else if you don't."

"I love them!" I say. "I can't wait to try them!"

She looks relieved. I get up to hug her, too. She jumps up and wraps her arms around me, then lifts me up and jostles me around in a giant hug, making my legs swing back and forth.

"You got heavy!" she says, putting me back down.

"OK, my turn now," my mom says.

My mom's gift bag is twice the size of Rory's and Gabe's.

"It's for the tree fort," she says. "The last finishing touch. I know the fort isn't perfect or *exactly* like you hoped. But I think we all did a pretty good job."

Inside is a box with a picture of a rope ladder on it.

I jump up and hug her. "This is exactly what I wanted! Thank you!"

"Once we set it up, we'll have to remove the temporary ladder," she says. "Then you'll really be able to keep intruders out."

"Can we do it now?" I ask.

"It's your birthday," my mom says. "We can do anything you want!"

I put my presents in one bag, sling it over my shoulder, and run outside to the fort. I scramble up the makeshift ladder my mom made, then carefully spread out my presents. "I'll get back to you later," I tell my sketchbook and new pens. Then I unpack the ladder box and follow the installation instructions. My mom taught me how to use most of the tools from my dad's old toolbox, so it's pretty easy. As soon as I'm done, I drop the ladder down and tug hard to make sure it's safe.

I peek through the hatch in the floor where Rory, Gabe, and my mom all wait below.

"Come on up!" I call.

"Let me test it first," my mom says. "I'm the heaviest." She starts to climb. The ladder swings a little bit, and she laughs at herself as she struggles. "This is more challenging than it looks!"

"Good!" I say. "That's how I want it to be!"

She makes it all the way up and squeezes through the hole. "I think it's good to go, Mapes!" she says.

When she calls me Mapes, it makes me think of my dad. He's usually the only one to call me that.

She ruffles my hair. "Dad will be so proud of you when he sees this," she says.

"What do you mean?" I ask. "Is he coming home? For my birthday?"

She frowns.

"Oh. Um. I'm sorry, honey. I just meant eventually."

I frown.

"Aw, honey. Don't let this spoil your day."

"How can I not? It's my birthday!"

"Maybe he'll call. It's only the morning. He could still call."

"He didn't write a song! He didn't do anything! He's the worst dad in the world!"

"What? Maple, no! Don't say that."

"It's true!" I say.

"Hey! What's going on up there?" Rory calls. The ladder shifts as she starts to climb up.

"Let's try to focus on the fun stuff today," my mom says. "It's OK to be angry with Dad. But don't let it spoil your birthday. Or try not to, anyway."

Rory's head pops through the hole. "It stinks that he's not here," she says. "But Mom's right. Don't let it ruin everything."

The rope tugs again as Gabe climbs up. Soon, we're all smooshed together in the fort. We sit side by side and look out at the view of the Ganders and the Brays.

"It sure is peaceful up here," my mom says.

"Lie down and look up at the branches," Rory says. "It's really cool!"

We all lie down and stare up at the tree. The wind gently rustles the bright green leaves. They whisper a little, and I imagine it's the tree's own birthday song to me.

Maybe my dad is sending me this message from a tree he's lying under right now. Maybe he's thinking of me after all. Maybe he misses me and wishes he could be here.

"I want to remember this moment forever," my mom says. "It's so wonderful to be here with you kids. I love you so much."

She reaches for my hand and holds it tight.

"It would be nicer if—" Gabe starts to say.

"Don't," Rory interrupts. "It doesn't need to be any nicer than this. It's fine just like this."

But I know what he was going to say. *If Dad was here. It would be nicer if Dad was here.*

We're all quiet for a long time, listening to the leaves whisper gently to us. If Dad was here, we'd be even more squished together. Maybe we wouldn't even all fit. But if Dad was here, this space would have been bigger. And there would be a roof and walls with windows. If Dad was here, he'd be singing a silly song and making me laugh and feel embarrassed but in a happy way.

But he's not here.

I don't even know where he is. Or what he's doing. Or if he even remembers it's my birthday.

"It's your birthday, time to par-tay," Rory sings quietly.

"Maple, Maple, shops at Staples," Gabe adds.

"She's a vision, doing division," my mom says.

I giggle.

"She's an artist and a fart-ist," Rory sings.

"Hey!" I yell.

Gabe makes a fart sound.

"It's your birthday, yay, yay, yay, yay," my mom sings.

"Yeesh, Mom, that's really the best you've got?" Gabe says.

My first thought is *We can't all be like Dad*. But I don't say it out loud, and I'm glad, because I know it would just hurt my mom's feelings and spoil the mood.

Besides, she answers Gabe's question by singing it again. Then Gabe and Rory join in.

"It's your birthday, yay, yay, yay, yay. It's your birthday, yay, yay, yay, yay."

It makes me feel good and a little sad at the same time. But mostly, it feels good.

Yay, yay, yay, yay.

Thirty-Two

We're all enjoying the moment, so we don't hear the sound of a car pull into the driveway. Or the sound of a door slam. We don't hear anything other than very bad singing until a voice cuts through our fun.

"Is my birthday girl up there?"

We all sit up.

"Dad?" Rory asks.

"Helloooooooooo!" he answers.

She peeks through the hole in the floor and yelps.

"It's Dad!" She scrambles out the hole and down the ladder.

Gabe follows.

My mom fixes her hair a little, then turns to me.

"You next," she says. She smiles, but it looks like it hurts.

"Did you know?" I ask.

She shakes her head. "Promise."

"You go first," I say.

She carefully squeezes through the hole and climbs down.

I peek through the hole and watch her struggle with the rope ladder. I wish she'd just used the other makeshift one. I don't want my dad to say something to hurt her feelings. But he doesn't say anything. When she steps onto the ground, he gives her a hug. It doesn't look like their usual hug. It definitely does not look like the kind of hug Oliver's parents give each other. It looks like a hug you give a relative you don't know very well. Awkward.

He peers up at me. "You coming down, Mapes?"

I nod and make my way to the ground. Before I reach the bottom rung, he wraps his arms around me and swoops me off the ladder.

"Happy birthday, kiddo! Oh, I missed you. You feel a whole year heavier!"

He smells different. His clothes don't smell like our usual laundry detergent. It's weird, and I don't like it. Also, he grew a beard.

He puts me down. "You didn't think I'd miss your birthday, did you, Mapes?"

I look at Mom, Rory, and Gabe, who all worked so hard to make the day special. Who even made up a song because my dad wasn't here to do it.

I shrug.

"Really, honey? Of course I wouldn't! Is that what you all thought?"

His good mood is gone already.

"You've been gone for weeks," Gabe says.

My mom reaches over and puts her hand on Gabe's shoulder. I don't know if it's to make him be quiet or to give him some love.

My dad runs his hand through his hair, which is also longer than usual. He glares at my mom.

"Didn't Mom explain to you we needed a little break?" he asks accusingly.

"Of course I did," my mom says.

"Then what's the problem?"

"Are you serious?" Gabe says so loudly, his voice cracks.

"Don't raise your voice at me!"

I step away from him and take my mom's free hand.

"Dad," Rory says. "We missed you."

His body seems to soften a little. "I missed you too, Ror. So much."

"You have a really odd way of showing it," Gabe says. "What's gotten into you?"

"What's gotten into me?" Gabe shrugs my mom's hand off his shoulder and steps out of her reach. "Are you really that clueless?"

"Gabe," my mom says. "Please don't."

"Please don't what? Act like this isn't normal? It's not! You left us, Dad! We had no idea how long you'd be gone. Mom had to do everything without you! We had to make Maple's tree fort without you! After you PROMISED her you'd do it. Again. We had to get by. WITHOUT YOU."

My dad shields his eyes and looks up at the fort. Through his eyes, I can see just how shabby it looks. The sides are uneven. The floor has gaps in it where the boards didn't quite fit together. The little blocks of wood my mom nailed up the tree to make a ladder are all different sizes and not lined up properly.

"Looks like you did a fine job. Without me," my dad says quietly.

"Please don't fight," Rory says. Her bottom lip starts to quiver. "I missed you, Dad." She rushes toward him and hugs him again.

"Glad someone did," he says.

Gabe rolls his eyes and stomps off toward the house, slamming the door when he goes inside.

The four of us stand there awkwardly.

"Do you want some breakfast?" my mom asks. "We made pancakes."

"I'm not hungry," my dad says. "C'mon, Mapes. Wanna show me your fort? Looks like you could use a hand still."

"It's finished," I say. "I just need to take down the ladder Mom made, now that I have my rope ladder."

"Finished? Don't you know a fort is never finished? There's always more to do!"

"I like it how it is," I say.

I can tell by the way his face changes that he knows I'm lying.

"Don't be stubborn, Maple," Rory says. "The fort could definitely use Dad's help."

"No!" I say. "It's done!" I march over to the toolbox we left under the tree and get a hammer, then start to pull the nails from the pieces of wood my mom attached. She was smart and made sure there was a bit of space between the nail head and the wood so the nails would be easy to pull out. I can feel the three of them watching me from behind. "I hope this doesn't hurt," I whisper to the tree before I start yanking. As soon as I begin, I feel my anger growing. We were having such a nice time, and my dad ruined it. He ruins everything!

After a while, I realize I haven't heard anyone talk. I turn around and see that they've all left. When I reach as high as I can from the ground, I climb the rope ladder and finish pulling out the final steps as I climb, dropping the pieces of wood to the ground as I go. My mom would say it's unsafe to leave wood around with nails sticking out, but I don't care. They look like little booby traps scattered on the ground, in case anyone tries to get near. When I finish and drop the last piece down, I squeeze through the hole and pull up the rope ladder.

There.

Now it really is *my* fort. No one can come up here unless I let the ladder down.

The leaves rustle above me, as if the tree approves. I reach over to touch the trunk that comes up through the floor, running my fingers along the bark. "I guess it's just us," I say, and lean my head on the solid, rough wood. "At least I know *you're* not going anywhere."

It's your birthday. Yay, yay, yay, yay.

Thirty-Three

"Helloooooo up there!" my dad's voice calls. "Is there a secret password or something I'm supposed to know?"

I close my sketchbook and peek through the hole in the floor.

My dad peers up at me. "I'm sorry about earlier. Can I come up?"

I hesitate. I missed him so much all this time he's been gone. So much it hurt. So why now that he's back do I want him to go away?

"I know you're upset, Mapes. I get it. Can't we talk about it?"

I squeeze the rope ladder in my hand.

"Honey, the last thing I wanted to do was spoil your birthday. I was hoping you'd want to see me. That's why I'm here. But if you want me to leave, I will."

My chest hurts where my heart is. How can someone love you and hurt you at the same time? If he loves us, why did he leave us? I guess the only way to find out is to ask.

I slowly drop the ladder down. He's so heavy that it creaks and groans when he starts to climb.

"What's the weight limit on this thing?" he asks. "I sure hope I don't break it!"

When he reaches the hole, he really has to squeeze through. The opening is so tight, it pulls on his shirt.

"Guess no big intruders will be getting in here!" he says when he finally manages to squeak through.

He crawls over to where I'm sitting and settles in next to me.

"Hi," he says.

"Hi."

"Nice view."

"Mm-hmm."

He pats the floor. "You all did a really nice job with this. Solid work."

I want him to stop talking.

"Guess you didn't need me after all, huh?"

The more he talks, the more that teakettle feeling starts to work itself up inside me. If he says one more thing, I'm going to let out some serious steam.

"I could help you build the third wa—"

"Stop!" I say. "Just SHUT UP! Please!"

He gasps.

"I'm sorry, but you're saying all the wrong things, Dad! I can't stand it!"

The pain on his face makes me feel awful, but I can't stop now.

"You *left* us, Dad! Like, you *left*! It was awful! We were so scared and sad. And now that you're back, you're acting like it was no big deal! But it was! People don't leave the ones they love. They don't!"

"Maple, I didn't—"

"Please stop talking, Dad! Please! You're making everything worse!"

I didn't realize I was crying until tears start to slip down my neck and onto my shirt.

My dad closes his eyes and takes a deep breath, as if he's trying to meditate or something.

Why is it that everything he does makes me so annoyed and mad?

"What do you want, honey?" he asks me. "I sincerely want to know."

I look out at the view and up at the branches overhead. The fort doesn't even have a roof. The leaves blow above us in the wind, making a *hush-hush-hush* sound.

"I don't know," I say. "I just want to sit here and be quiet, I guess."

"All right, honey. I can do that."

Side by side, we lean back and sit quietly. I wonder if he likes this view better than whatever view he had at Peter's cabin.

My tears keep coming. They just drip and drip down my face and onto my T-shirt. I let them out. I let them out and out and out until I run out of them. When I look over at my dad, I realize he's done the same thing.

"Why did you leave, Dad?" I finally ask. "I know sometimes we get to be too much for you, but to just leave without even saying goodbye, for days, is wrong."

"I know. And I'm sorry."

"But why did you do it?"

"I knew it was best for everyone. I was disappointing your mom and losing my temper when she got after me about it. And I didn't want to do that in front of you kids. I didn't want you all to see that side of me. I should have explained before I left. You're right. But it has nothing to do with you kids. Your mom and I . . . well, we . . ."

He doesn't seem to know what to say, so I save him the trouble. "Are you getting divorced?"

It's the question I've been wondering for a long time now. Even though I'm afraid of the answer, I decide it's more important to know.

He doesn't answer right away, and that makes me feel a little scared.

"I don't know the answer to that question," he finally says. "I'm sorry."

"You don't love her anymore, do you?"

"Why would you say that?"

"Because before you left, you said a lot of awful things to her."

He sighs. "I know. I'm sorry."

"Did you tell her that?"

"Not yet. But I will. You kids sure do look out for your mother," he says, kind of chuckling.

I cross my arms at my chest. I'm starting to feel frustrated with him all over again. Doesn't he get that this isn't funny? Why can't he just try? Why can't he be like Old Dad instead of Dadlandia Dad?

"I'm sorry, Mapes. It's just . . . this is hard for me. It's hard for me to explain without sounding like a selfish jerk. But sometimes, couples grow apart. Even when they love each other, they just . . . stop feeling the same way. They still love each other, but they aren't *in love*. Little things start to annoy them about each other. Pretty soon, they don't want to be around each other anymore." He doesn't say this in a sad way, just a matter-of-fact way.

I think about Oliver's parents and how *in love* they seem. Why can't my mom and dad be like that? Why does my dad have to be the opposite of a magnet?

"Why can't you both stop doing the things that annoy each other?" I ask. "Is it really that hard? Can't you at least try?"

He smiles. "I think it's more complicated than that."

"Seems easy to me. Seems like you're just too lazy. Or you don't care enough."

"Well, you're ten. I mean eleven! It will make more sense when you're older."

I push away from him. "Stop talking to me like I'm a baby! I'm serious, Dad. We need to know if you're coming back for good. Don't you care how being away affects me? And Rory and Gabe? And Mom?"

He sighs dramatically. "Well, I'm here right now. Doesn't that show I care?"

I shrug. It's not enough. And I bet he knows that just as well as I do.

"Maybe you care right now, but what about tomorrow?"

"Mapes, I will *always* care."

"I wish you had a better way of showing it."

"Ouch," he says. "That's harsh."

There are so many things I want to say, like *So is leaving your family and sending pathetic little texts to tell us to be good!* But instead, I just shrug again. What's the point?

He scooches forward and starts to squeeze himself back through the hole in the floor. "Let me know if you want help fixing this place up," he says.

"I won't," I say. "It's perfect the way it is."

He squeezes out and disappears without a reply. As soon as the ladder goes slack, I pull it back up. Then I start to cry all over again.

Thirty-Four

"Ahoy there!" a voice calls from below.

I'm not sure how long it's been since my dad left, but I do know my bum is sore from sitting so long. I look down at my unfinished comic. "To be continued, I guess," I whisper.

I tuck my sketchbook and supplies back in the bag, crawl over to the hole, and peek down.

Staring up at me are Charlie, Katy, Astrid, and the whole Rainbow crew. Adam, Bryce, and Dora are here, too.

"Surprise!" Astrid says.

I release the ladder and climb down.

"What are you all doing here?" I ask.

"It's your birthday! Your mom invited us."

"She did?"

"Yup!"

I realize now they are all wearing rainbow flowers. Oliver has one wrapped around each button of his shirt, so he looks like a clown. Charlie has a bunch looped together to look like a big necklace. Dora has one tied around each of her pigtails. She steps forward and hands me a string of flowers and motions for me to bend down, then places it on my head so it fits perfectly around my crown, which I forgot I was wearing!

Rory and Gabe push through the back door with a tray of food and a cake, which they bring to the old picnic table in the corner of the yard.

The cake is covered with rainbow flowers.

"The cake is my birthday present to you," Oliver says. "My dad and I made it because I remember how much you liked the one I had at my party."

"Wow!" I say. "It's amazing!"

"Can I go get the presents?" Dora asks me.

"Presents?"

"They're in the driveway," Katy explains. "Because of the surprise."

Dora runs off and comes back pulling a wagon full of gifts.

I can't believe this is happening.

My mom and dad come out next, with more bowls of food. My mom is beaming, but my dad looks sad. It makes me feel bad. I know I hurt his feelings earlier. But

I wanted him to know how I felt. How we all felt. I just wish it would make a difference.

"What's with all the flowers?" my dad asks.

Denzel walks over to my dad and hands him one without answering.

"What do I do with it?"

"Wear it in your own unique way," Carmella says.

"Rainbows make you happy," Oliver says.

My dad ties the flower around his wrist and pretends to smell it. He looks surprised when he discovers it actually has a scent.

"Is that coconut?" he asks.

"Probably," Denzel says. "We currently have four different scents, but we're adding more each week." He gives my mom a flower.

She ties it around her wrist just like my dad did, then sniffs.

"Vanilla?" she asks. "Mmmmm. That's nice."

"I love how it smells when my dad bakes," Oliver explains. "So I borrowed some extracts to make scented water. Then I sprayed the flowers lightly with it."

"Clever!" my dad says.

"I have a mind for business," Oliver says. "Someday, I hope to be an entrepreneur. This is just . . ." He hesitates. "Practice. To see how the product is received by the general public."

"Oh! Are you the kid who had the business-themed birthday?"

"Correct."

Gabe asks Denzel for a flower and sniffs. "Orange!" he says. He ties it to a belt loop by his hip. I wonder if he and my dad made up. It seems so. At least, Gabe seems in a better mood.

Rory puts a big flower on the back belt loop of her shorts and hops around. "Bunny tail!" she explains.

"Your sister is funny," Dora tells me.

"I have a whole list of games I invented to teach you all," Rory says. "So let's get this party started!"

"Warning," I tell the group. "Rory's games are not like most games."

"That's right!" Rory says. "My games are for brave souls who enjoy competition!"

"Oh dear," my mom says. Then she can't seem to help herself. "Someone's gonna end up cry-ing," she sings softly.

I look over at my dad to see if it annoyed him, but he's busy smiling, one arm over Gabe's shoulder. They definitely made up!

Rory takes off toward the Ganders. "Follow me!" she calls. They all start to chase after her, even Gabe and my dad.

"Mom," I say, taking her hand to keep her back for a minute. "Did you plan all this?"

"Your brother and sister did," she says, putting her other hand on my shoulder. "I just helped."

"Thank you," I say.

"I'm glad your birthday turned out so special after all, honey. I know it probably wasn't easy, seeing your dad when you weren't expecting it."

"No. It wasn't."

"Are you happy that he came?"

It seems like she wants me to say yes, but I don't want to lie to her. I don't know how I feel. Is it wrong to be disappointed in your own dad?

"You don't have to answer," she tells me. "It's a complicated feeling, isn't it?"

I nod.

We watch everyone chase Rory in the distance, trying to grab her flower tail. The Ganders squawk at her from their side of the fence. I wonder if she'll dare any of my friends to race them.

"It's nice to see all your friends here," my mom says. "I seem to recall you didn't used to like the triplets very much. What did you call them?"

"The ABC's," I say. "They used to be annoying, but they're nice now."

"People change," my mom says. "Sometimes for the better."

"But sometimes for the worse. Like Dad," I blurt out.

"Please don't say that, honey," she says sadly.

"But it's true."

She shakes her head. "It's not that simple."

"Please don't tell me I'm too young to understand."

"I wasn't going to. I promise. I just don't want you to be mad at Dad. *People* are complicated. All of us. But your dad loves you kids more than anything. He was doing what he thought was best for our family. He didn't want you kids hearing us fight all the time."

"Why do you have to fight, anyway?"

"Oh, I don't know, honey. It's—"

"Complicated."

"Mm-hmm. Dad has a lot of pressure at work. He has a lot of pressure at home. Raising a family is hard. There's so much responsibility. Sometimes when you're overwhelmed, you take it out on people you love. Or you blame them. Sometimes, you just really need a break. Dad and I are going to figure all of this out. I don't know what that will look like, but I promise we are both trying. But today is your special day. Can't we talk about something happier? Like rainbow flowers?" She sniffs the flower at her wrist. "Your friend Oliver sure is a character."

I adjust my rainbow headband. "You should see his house. It's like . . . perfect. He has a tree house with real glass windows and everything!" I don't tell her he also has perfect parents. And clothes. And his own bedroom. And an office.

"That sounds nice," she says, looking up at our makeshift fort. "I wish I could have helped you make the fort of your dreams."

I reach for her hand. "It's OK, Mom. I like my fort."

"You do?"

"Yeah. It's . . . perfectly imperfect."

"Ha! Where'd you get such a big vocabulary, anyway?"

"Astrid!"

She bumps me with her hip. "I'm glad you have such special friends."

I realize they really are special. Even the ABC's. Maybe if they can change for the better, Dad can, too.

I hug my mom around the waist and squeeze as hard as I can without hurting her. "I love you," I say. "I love you so much!"

"Honey!" she says, surprised. "I love you, too! Now go have fun. But don't get hurt!"

I turn and grin at her before I race off. "What's a little goose?" I say, and wiggle my bum.

She laughs and shakes her head.

I adjust my paper flower headband and take off. "Wait for me!" I call, running to catch up with my friends. I feel like a queen. Queen for a day. That's what my mom always tells us on her birthday.

As I get close, I can see my dad talking to the Ganders and my friends all laughing. Rory is balancing on top of the fence, explaining the rules of some game she's invented. Gabe shakes his head at her, as if to warn her she's gone too far and someone really is going to end up crying. But then he starts laughing and hopping up and down like a goofball. I smile, relieved to see him not angry anymore.

Everyone looks happy, covered in rainbow flowers. It makes me feel happy, too. Happier, maybe, than I've ever felt. I don't know what's going to happen next. Not with my mom and dad. Not with my friends. Not with my comics. Not with anything, really. Things are always changing. People are always changing. Sometimes in special, wonderful ways. And sometimes not. But right now, the people I love are covered in good-smelling flowers, laughing, and playing together. I try to take a picture of it in my mind, so I can draw them later and remember this moment forever.

It's your birthday!
YAY!

ACKNOWLEDGMENTS

Once again, I am forever thankful for the wise, kind, and steady guidance of my editor, Joan Powers, who is endlessly patient and generous. Thank you also to Glynnis Fawkes, who agreed to give Maple's comics life and love. As always, to my writing partners and dear friends Debbi Michiko Florence and Cindy Faughnan, for their valuable feedback and determination to help me over the finish line time and again. To my husband, Peter Carini, for doing the same, and so much more. To my agent, Jennifer Laughran, for taking me on during a difficult time in my life. To my mom and dad, Judi and Malcolm Knowles, who texted me from their vacation several years ago and announced they had the perfect title for my next book. You guys didn't think I'd take on the challenge, but here you go! And finally, to the wonderful people of Team Candlewick for the dedication and love you all put into making and promoting books for young people. Thank you for the important work you do.